Moving Waters

STORIES BY

Racelle Rosett

Print ISBN 9780786752850
eISBN 9780786752928

"The False Bride" first appeared in *Tikkun*. "Levi" first appeared in *Moment Magazine*. "The Unveiling" first appeared in *Lilith*. "New Jew" first appeared in *Zeek*. "Shomer" first appeared in *New Vilna Review*. "T'shuva" first appeared in *Jewish Fiction*. "Moving Waters" first appeared in *Santa Monica Review*.

Cover design by Charlotte Strick
Jacket Painting by William Deutsch

Distributed by
Argo Navis Author Services
www.argonavisdigital.com

For my sons,
Daniel Sawyer and David Isaac

Contents

Moving Waters

WINTER BLOOM didn't plan to fall in love with the nanny of her son's classmate. She was married, for one thing, and, a moment before straight, or at least she was until she saw the cotton straps of the nanny's sundress tied at the top of her suntanned shoulders and thought, in full, of what it would be like to untie them. The nanny's parents were Israeli, well, had tried to be, had lived for seven months in a dusty flat in Be'er Sheva, before turning around and going back to their teaching jobs in upstate New York, but not before naming their daughter Aviva, which meant Spring. Winter, whose parents had named her Susan—a name she relinquished when ordering her first set of head shots—could not stop thinking of the way their names rhymed and whether or not, at this late date, she might yet qualify as a lesbian. She had experimented once, some thirty years before in college, with a girl across the hall in the dorm, who was now an agent at ICM and would tell the story from time to time to her husband to get him hard. Winter was nearly fifty, and wasn't sure that the girl—she was certainly a girl—would find her beautiful in return. At the gym, Winter increased her time on the elliptical from thirty to forty-five minutes. And when she thought of her—this highly paid nanny who had a master's in Jewish Folklore—she thought of how soft her mouth would be. And then, one afternoon at the Grove, she found out.

They had taken the boys to see a movie, and afterward they had stopped at the Fresh store. There, while the boys sampled fragrances just underfoot, Aviva tested a lip-gloss called Burnt Sugar. "It's pretty," Winter said.

"It would look good on you too," said Aviva, and with that Aviva leaned over and pressed the color from her lips onto Winter's. And from that moment, Winter was unable to do the smallest thing—drop off her son at carpool, pick him up in the same line six hours later—without longing for her, the nanny of the single mother who was a writer on the hit medical series developed for television by Winter's husband, Howie.

Twice when she had sex with her Howie, Winter's thoughts drifted to Aviva—easy images of her shoulders, her hair pulled back at her neck—Winter only carried back to the here-and-now by the scruff of her husband's chin or the deep resonance of his voice. Winter wondered if the thoughts themselves were adulterous. She was sure that any ladies magazine would back her play and remind her that fantasy is healthy and can enhance the sex life of a couple married nearly twenty years. But that was not what she was feeling. She was feeling that, in the same way that she had organized her thinking around a successful career, and then again to raise her child, that within her, something was stirring. That busily in the back and sometimes the front of her mind, a direction was being taken; that while she pushed her cart around Whole Foods, she was winding her way out of her marriage.

A screenwriter friend, who had been twenty-five years sober when he went back to drinking, owned the Case Study house that Winter wanted. She was fairly certain that she could acquire it with the money in her residual account from her first sitcom. The screenwriter's soon to be ex-wife was liquidating his assets, having already sold his collection of first editions and then moving onto the quirky parade of vintage typewriters that marched around the perimeter of his office. He had restarted his drinking with a commitment to Warner Bros., who had paid for the first and second rehab. Before the third, the studio had sued his wife for the story payment and the rent of his office on the lot. Winter's business manager, Victor, contacted the writer's wife and made the offer. It was fair and accepted without counter, a *mitzvah* really, helping the wife out of a bind. And although Winter's heart ached thinking of her son joining the ranks of Wednesday and every other Sunday travelers, she knew that divorce no longer held the stigma that it used to, certainly not here in LA, and that her new place was architecturally significant and had a tidy little bedroom near hers where she could hear Noah sleep, although most nights he still climbed in with her, sleepyheaded, like a puppy. She would lift the blanket like the door of a tent for him to tuck inside—the smell of his hair still a drug to her.

Winter drove her husband to the San Ysidro Ranch to tell him, in the very room where they had stayed only four days after they met on the set of the first short-lived *Ellen* series. With their names wood-burned into a plaque outside the door for the last time, Winter told Howie that she loved him and their lives together, but that there was only one life, as far as she knew, and that she needed hers to be authentic. They both cried and held each other. They made love slowly and powerfully in a way that made Winter suspect that she wasn't the only one imagining her new life with Aviva.

Winter bought lean, modern furniture for the spare, beautiful house, and when her son was with his father, Aviva would bring her things from her place in Los Feliz and spend the night. In the mornings, they would lounge on the sofa with the *New York* and *Los Angeles Times* and Winter would watch Aviva as she walked to the kitchen for more coffee, nearly always in a white tank and Cosabella panties in the colors of sherbet.

Winter surprised herself at how facile she was in their lovemaking, like discovering a hidden talent, like waking up one day and finding you can draw. She loved the aesthetic of sex with Aviva, who was immaculate and had skin that smelled of products from the store where they first kissed—milk, nectarine, sugar—her skin as firm and warm as a newly baked yellow cake. Winter liked the way Aviva's hand felt in hers and how she leaned into her flirtatiously, even when they had been together six months and flew back east to Aviva's parents' house in Woodstock for Passover. Aviva's mother was about the same age as Winter, but so skilled at being without judgment, that she sat up late with her and talked about the Israeli authors they liked in common: Amos Oz, David Grossman, and, in the morning when Winter and Aviva slept together in Aviva's childhood room, pulled the door closed for them so they could have privacy. When they awoke together in the sun filled room, Winter drew the white sheets over her head and, with Aviva biting her lip, had nearly silent sex, while Aviva's parents prepared Matzoh Brei a room away.

After the requisite cooling off period that allowed her to now finalize her divorce in the state of California, Winter and Howie, names that never rhymed, sat at the table in an office in Century City, in a room with a Hockney collage of people playing cards, and, with hyperbolic generosity, divided the Haywood Wakefield furniture and the posters by Robbie Conal, the Roy McMakin desk, the box at the Bowl, stepping over each other with consideration as if vying for the title of best divorce ever. Howie's parents had managed their divorce less well, treating it as a blood sport. He had vowed to do better, for Noah. Even when it hurt him, even when he wished to raise his voice, he smoothed it instead like the white sheets of a bed. The rancorless division was admirable, and in the elevator, Winter unconsciously pet the sleeve of Howie's shirt. His kiss on her cheek at the valet was soft and proprietary.

Howie had quickly taken to the habit of including Aviva when considering Winter's weekend plans. "Where are you and Aviva staying in Santa Barbara? Be sure and take Aviva to see the Murakami," creating room for Aviva, the fact of her, as if she were a gift for both of them, like a thoughtful exchange student who replenished the milk and sometimes lingered to dry the dishes. But in all his consolation and obedience, Howie had been reluctant to give Winter a *get*—Howie, who after twenty years, had just begun to believe that Winter was his, who had still not recovered from the first surprise that she had agreed to go out with him—not out really—but back to his house in the hills after the taping of the pilot, where she sat in his Eames chair with her hands tucked into her sleeves and her knees to her chest, while he made her cocoa like an after school snack. She was far more beautiful to him with her face scrubbed and hair pulled back, than coiffed and made up for the show. In the morning, when he saw her come out of his bedroom in his sweats held up with one hand at her waist, he thought he would die. He had handed her coffee. Taking the mug with a peacock logo, she released her hold on the sweats, which fell easily to the floor. She sipped her coffee, looking up at him over the rim, set it back down, hopped onto the counter and unbuttoned her shirt. When Noah was born, he admitted that what he did at work mattered to him very little, but for the world he could make for his family. He regarded his wife and son as a dream woken up to.

In the end, Rabbi Beth, who had also married them, had had to call him in like a truant Bar Mitzvah student. Howie had dragged himself to her office, and then, like a child in a backyard play, commanded the scribe to, in real-time, draft the divorce proclamation. Howie and Winter were taken to separate rooms to wait, literally, for the ink to dry. Aviva had taken their son to the Tar Pits and, from the window of the empty classroom where she waited, Winter pretended to herself that she could see them: Noah only willing and delighted to be driven to school by Aviva, to be helped at the dining room table with his spelling list, and to have milk poured by her into his cereal. Winter calculated that, right about now, they would be in the gift shop buying worthless Tar Pit swag. She would have to remind Aviva about saying no. Winter wished that she and Howie had not been separated while they waited. She remembered when, late in her pregnancy with Noah, she had begun cramping. She was frightened, and that bitch, Dr. Davidson, had made Howie wait outside. She felt embarrassed to want him near her now, to help her leave him, weak in a way that she sometimes felt with him. The cute rabbinical intern, who looked like an even younger Ashton Kutcher, leaned the door open with a silent *ta-dah* and let Winter know it was time.

In the rabbi's office, Winter was instructed to extend her hands, palms up, in front of her like for a mother wrapping a skein of wool. Winter stared up at Howie, surprised to see tears welling in his eyes. He drew his breath as if to reverse the tears, and proceeded to lay the document in her hands. Winter was instructed to take steps away from him as he pronounced the words that released her. Moments later, the corners were torn from the document and it was placed on file. The rabbis' secretary, Marilyn, stopped them in the outer office and cheerfully reminded Howie and Winter of the meeting next Sunday for selecting a date for their son's Bar Mitzvah, which was three years away. Howie righted himself and, drawing his finger across its face, entered the information into his iPhone. In the parking lot, Howie hugged Winter briskly and got quickly into his car, where she could see that, once again, he was crying, and as he pulled away, she stood with her keys in her hands looking for them. Winter glanced back at where she had just been and then down at her hands, and wondered how the keys had come to be there. Inside the car, suddenly weary, she shut her eyes and did not open them again until she heard the voice of the eager intern on the heels of the rabbi. It was dusk, and hers was the only car left in the lot. Winter started her car and rolled it past the security guard who, ducking down, looked at her carefully and then waved back.

With the divorce and *get* now final, Winter drove west on Mulholland for her appointment at the U of J Mikvah. Winter had removed her nail polish as the email from the Mikvah Lady had instructed, and, wearing flip-flops for the pedicure she had scheduled for immediately afterward, downshifted into a lower gear so that she would not go careening off the cliff into the ravine like the half-a-dozen drivers that did so every year. Winter had made the appointment at the University of Judaism at the suggestion of Rabbi Beth. The idea of a *mikvah* seemed strange to Winter at first, a throwback to the idea of family purity, when women were *tameh*—impure—and needed to immerse before returning to their husbands, a bride again. But Rabbi Beth had assured her that it was different now, that it was part of the empowerment of women to take this ritual back. Winter had hesitated at first, but came around after talking to her friend Mayim, who had once worked as Winter's double and was now a life coach. Her left hand firmly on the wheel, Winter cranked up the Yael Naim CD Aviva had given her—everything about Aviva, new and of the moment.

Winter parked the car up on the top of the hill and walked past the gift shop to the elevator and down to the Mikvah office. She had been there once before on a tour with Rabbi Beth and the Sisterhood. She had learned that, to satisfy the edict that a *mikvah* must run with moving waters, a panel of scholars in Los Angeles had arrived at the inventive solution of bringing in blocks of ice, which, when melted, were sanctified. Winter hadn't told anyone that she was coming, not even Aviva, and told her instead she was going to Pilates. Surprised, but not distressed by her own omission, Winter reminded herself that relationships need breath to survive. She walked past the school bulletin board that offered Hebrew tutoring and a room to share, a reward for a lost watch, scholarships to a school in the Negev. She tore off a little white slip for a Jewish sleep-away in Ojai, thinking it might be good for Noah.

In the Mikvah office, a woman with wet hair, who seemed more religious than Winter, was writing a check to the woman at the desk, who Winter assumed was Sharona, the woman she had spoken to on the phone. Sharona acknowledged Winter with a broad smile and continued her conversation with the woman whose skirt landed well below her knees and whose shirt covered her arms and rose high on her throat. To dress that way in LA was to be Amish. Winter tucked her naked feet in flip-flops under the chair. The woman made her feel out of place and that she might have made a mistake. Sharona guided the woman to the door, her hand at her elbow, and lingered there for a moment speaking quietly, a reassurance that Winter could sense but not hear. On the table, Winter saw a book of photographs of women in blue water, their hair floating around them like lithe seaweed. She was about to reach for it when the Amish Jewess took her leave. Sharona clapped her hands, startling Winter to her feet. "Susan," she said. Winter blushed at the sound of her given name. Sharona had the energy of a teacher on the first day of school. Winter took a half step toward her with her hand extended, but Sharona closed the gap and embraced her. The embrace was not cursory. Rather, Sharona held her, breathing deliberately in and exhaling. Winter surprised herself by giving way to it. She felt her feet sink and her body relax. Sharona rocked back and looked at Winter with the pride and pleasure of a parent, "Why are you here?"

Winter, without thinking, told the truth. "My marriage," she began, then, "I've...I'm divorced." Sharona opened her self out, but did not let go of Winter's hand. Sharona nodded, and Winter saw that she was grieving. Like her husband's tears, she wondered at this woman who did not even know her, but had taken the full weight of the divorce as if it were her own failure. But even as Winter watched her, Sharona recovered, as if placing the loss in an in-box, a tickler file to review later. Sharona released Winter's hand in a way that now felt abrupt, and pressed open a door to a changing area that, in every way, resembled the one at Kinara Spa. On the wall was a list of steps that Sharona read aloud with the mixed routine and vigilance of a flight attendant. Any missed step would make the immersion unkosher. Winter listened now attentively. She was to use the bathroom, shower, remove her jewelry, brush and floss, rinse her mouth, and, with a Q-tip, trace the shape of her ear, as she had done so carefully for baby Noah. When she had completed the tasks, she was to comb her hair through and squeeze it, but not dry it. She was to stand at the door and knock, and Sharona would come for her.

Alone in the room, Winter felt like a schoolgirl, referring to her notes hoping to do well. As she stood in her bare feet, the pink of her nail beds unfamiliar to her, not polished to the gloss of a car. She felt a million miles away from the rest of LA on her secret mission. If there were an earthquake, no one would know where to look for her. She removed her rings and set them on the sink. The wedding band had come from Barneys and was a Reinstein Ross, which, she was reasonably sure, meant Ross Reinstein, a nice Jewish boy in the jewelry business. It was too nice not to wear. The band was rose gold and with it was a diamond-seeded ring by the same artist. Howie had gotten the ring for her when Noah was born, to mark the courageous day when, at Cedars, she had delivered him in a room with Howie's parents and brother Seth, the color TV mounted on the wall showing a Lakers game, and a buffet of sandwiches from Canter's for everyone but her. Howie's mom, Elaine, who had wished for a daughter after a lifetime of boys, had braced Winter's knee against her shoulder when it was time to push.

Winter put the rings on the stem of the toothbrush they had given her, and left it on the counter, reasoning that a person who stole from a *mikvah* would have to be pretty bold. She wrapped the towel, tucked it in over her left breast and, curling the toes of her bare feet under, knocked as she'd been told to, on the door.

Sharona opened it as if she had always been behind it, and silently brought Winter into the cobalt tiled room. Winter was led by Sharona with the measured steps of a bride. The water was as blue as the pool itself—a pool for one—with seven steps descending and a guide rail leading down. A small cistern that housed the melting ice was side by side and, connecting them, Sharona explained, was a small stopper that, when opened, allowed a *nishika* of water, a kiss. Sharona guided Winter to the top of the stairs, took the towel from Winter as prescribed, and, in deference to Winter's modesty, held the towel in front of her own eyes, so that she could only see the top of Winter's head as she descended. Winter took the first step down and found the water not cool as she had expected, but temperate like the days in LA when the air temperature is so close to that of your own body that you can't discern it, feeling only that you are buoyed through your day.

Sharona read to her from a script, but Winter's attention to it went in and out, attending more to the thoughts that ran through her mind in the darkened room like the illuminated screen of a drive-in. She remembered being married, not the wedding, but an hour before at their place on Hauser, when she and Howie had stolen away to the stairwell that led to their back porch and he had hiked her dress and pulled aside her blue silk panties to enter her, hoisting her by the ass and leaning her against the cool painted wall. She stepped again, and the water rose to her calves. She remembered bathing Noah in the sink, when he was so small and she so fearful, that every gesture was rhymed with an apology. "I'm sorry, I'm sorry, I'm sorry," she said as she cradled his trusting head in her hands. Howie, the more skilled at swaddling, waited with a duck-billed towel.

Sharona was reminding Winter to let go of past hurts as the water grazed her thighs, and this seemed too much to ask. Instead, she surprised herself by praying that she would have the strength to do it. To pray seemed a strange thing to her, so long had she gotten everything she wanted. She took the next two stairs one after another and her fingertips traced the surface of the pool. Winter looked at her navel as it pooled with water. Howie would follow the curve of it with his hand, asking her, like a man with a fetish, to do fewer crunches so that it would not be rock hard; coming up from behind her when she would try to read a script, vying for her attention like a child. When, at the sixth step, the water lifted her breasts, she remembered them full in her pregnancy, the unrivaled pleasure of nursing her son, the cup of his rosebud mouth, robust in his sucking. Rarely had she felt so proud.

At the bottom step, the water came above Winter's shoulders, and the surprising pressure of the surrounding water caused her to panic and her heart to pound. She reached for the pool's edge. Sharona crouched down beside her. "It's all right," she said, "You'll get used to it in a second." She nodded her head and Winter relaxed her breathing. Sharona continued her instructions. "It helps to jump up a little, just a little hop." Winter tentatively removed her hand from the wall. She felt better now, but still shaken. On tiptoe, the water was up to her neck. "A little hop, that will help you go completely under." Winter stepped away from the wall, and, centering herself in the pool, found that she was trembling, her breath stuttering as she exhaled, like an unfamiliar stage fright. Winter focused on Sharona's instructions, "A little hop," she reminded her. Winter obeyed her, and jumping, she dropped back into the water. Floating there, her back rising from the air in her lungs, she slowly exhaled and, splayed her fingers, the way that Sharona had demonstrated. Then, dropping her feet and lifting her face, she drew in a breath and looked up at Sharona. "Kosher," she pronounced. Winter laughed, relieved. "And again." Winter, now expert, repeated the immersion twice more. Sharona guided her through the blessings that were printed at the pool's edge in transliterated Hebrew. And then, leaving her alone, reminded her that the prayers uttered in a *mikvah* were carried most swiftly to God. Winter looked after her, wanting to follow, afraid to be alone.

Winter relaxed her body with intention and reminded herself that it was only a pool, that there was nothing in particular to be afraid of. She focused on the physical details around her; the way in a scary movie she would divert herself by training her eyes on the exit sign. It was tile and water, the candles were candles, she was fairly certain that the dish of potpourri was from Bed Bath and Beyond. She let her head tip back into the water her arms drift out to her sides. "Noah," she heard herself say, as easy as breathing. She already felt him moving away from her. She remembered the longing she had felt when he was an infant, how she betrayed herself daily loving the Noah he was, even as the Noah he'd only just been receded. She had read Wendy Mogel's *The Blessing of a Skinned Knee*, and knew that she needed to let him falter and stand away that he might learn to stand, that she was to not build his dioramas or manage his play dates, but let him be his own ten-year-old man. She had nearly bragged that he'd gotten through the divorce just fine. She had arranged for five visits with the doctor *LA Magazine* had named best family therapist, so that he could express his anger, and when it was her week, she would sit in the waiting area, re-reading the lone issue of *Martha Stewart Living*, reminding herself to someday serve pumpkin soup in a pumpkin. Noah would come out hoisting his backpack, his Buckley uniform disheveled from a day of play, his knees scuffed, all boy. Together, they would go to Ben and Jerry's at the Galleria, and over Oreo sundaes, he would ask her like a perfect gentlemen how her day was, telling her only that school was "fine," giving Winter nothing to work with, no truths to share like in the second act of her sitcom, where levity would halt for meaningful feelings and she would tousle the hair of whatever twin played her son that day. He resisted her maternal concerns and, looking daily more like Howie, seemed bent on protecting her. More and more, father and son soldiered on. She thought of them as she had seen them together in the sanctuary.

It was a Friday night service and she and Howie had been seated on either side of him; Howie, after work, with his jacket folded on the empty seat beside him, a closed prayer book on his lap. Rabbi Snow had invited, to come up for an *aliyah*, anyone who had gone through a transition in the year prior: a new home, a new job, and then, he had quipped, "a divorce," and under the cover of the congregation's laughter, Winter had leapt to her feet. Grabbing a *tallis*, she had made her way giddily up to the *bima*, and as she climbed the stairs, she had seen her son, seen him resting on the shoulder of his father, as a weary swimmer on the shore. His feet were tucked up under him like a younger child and he regarded her, his mother. He regarded her not with judgment or rancor. He regarded her without even curiosity. He regarded her as if she were only familiar. Someone he might have known, but in the end did not know. And then, he closed his eyes and, shifting his weight, rested against the body of his father. His father, who had not left him, who had not let a cold wind steal into their home. His father, who was still his parent, with whom he had the contract of boat and harbor. Howie, had reached for his jacket and brought it around Noah's small shoulders, then rested his arm across the boy's back. Winter had had to be shaken by Ellie Herman, who had quit television that year to write a book, and who had hustled Winter up the remaining stairs. The rabbi had held up the laminated prayers and Winter had recited them, hearing her own voice distantly.

Winter felt the chill of the water at the back of her neck. Her arms floated at her sides like a drowner. Her breath shallow, nearly silent. First drawing in a breath through her nose, and breathing out her mouth, Winter softened her knees and brought them to her chest and, letting go, dropped easily below the surface of the pool, with water touching every part of her body, no part of her exposed to air.

And then, pressing her feet fast to the tile bottom, Winter brought her face to the surface and refilled her lungs with air. She wiped the water from her eyes with her hands. Then, steadying herself with one hand on the ledge, she used the other to trace the cistern wall, locating the stopper that connected the two pools, and bracing herself, turned it hard counter-clockwise to stop the moving waters. Turning away, she took hold of the metal rails and hoisted herself out of the water, taking the stairs two at a time. She wrapped herself again in the towel against the cool air; patted her face, and then, bending, briskly dried her feet, first one and then the other so that she would not slip. She took quick small steps across the wet tile floor, resisting the urge to run.

Levi

THERE ARE SEVENTY-TWO disturbing images on the way to my school. *Saw I, Saw II, Two and Half Men.* There is a billboard for jeans in which no one is wearing clothes. I don't know why there isn't a law about this. In another billboard there was a picture of a woman with a plastic tube up her nose. Her eyes were red and bruised underneath. My mother gasped and called the billboard company, CBS Outdoor, right from her car. My friend Gabriel's mother called too, and I guess about a hundred or so other mothers, because the next day in the *LA Times* there was an article saying the billboards were coming down. On Highland, they had the tube-in-the-nose billboard three times, so that even if I was very fast and looked down at my shoes, when I looked up again it was there three more times and another hundred or so times in my mind the rest of the day. Good morning tube-in-her-nose take out your pencils tube-in-her-nose today we're going to learn tube-in-her-nose, tube-in-her-nose, tube-in-her-nose. Underneath the picture was the word torture, like what they did at Abu Ghraib, the prison in Iraq, because George Bush told them to. I hate George Bush most of all. My doctor, who is a cognitive therapist, who is six feet six inches tall and looks like John Heder, but more handsome (my mother says), told me to use thought-stopping techniques when this happens. He told me to imagine a stop sign crashing down into my brain, which is a disturbing image all by itself. I am identified highly gifted. My mother says that being gifted doesn't mean that the gift is yours, it means that the gift is for the world and it is given through you, that you are chosen to carry the gift. Sometimes I feel like I have a giant chicken on my back.

My name is Levi. I can play any music that I want. My mother bought our piano with the residuals from the TV show she worked on, and even thought I wasn't born yet, she said that she bought it for me. She said that if she put it in the living room and I walked by it every day, that one day I would sit down and play it, and that's what happened. I was meant to have an older brother, but he was too gentle for the world, and on the day he was supposed to be born, he died instead and went back to heaven. I have been to his grave. It says, "Hello, I must be going," from Groucho Marx, a famous Jewish comedian. When you go to the place where my brother is buried, you can see the big hat at the Disney Animation building. Walt Disney did not like Jews. My brother's name is Natan, which means a gift, so I guess I carry him too.

My school is actually my temple. We have three security guards: Troy, Ray and Gus. They are there because not everybody likes Jews. It is for the same reason we take off our shoes at the airport, because if they mean to, my mom says, people will do harm. She says we have to live our life anyway, that in the spring, we have to go to Israel on a plane. She took a bowl of sugar and put a tiny fleck of pepper in it. "This is the whole sweet world," she said, "and this," she points to the tiny fleck of pepper, "is the danger." She let me taste the sugar on the end of my finger. In Israel, people get onto buses with bombs taped to themselves and blow up everyone. There are special religious people who gather up the parts of the people to put back together so they can bury them. This is the job of someone. When my brother died, a person sat next to him and said prayers all night and day. That is someone's job too. My parents are television writers. They do not let me see the news or read the paper but you can find things out. Once, at Kennedy Airport, I was so scared they wouldn't let me on the plane until my mother gave me half her Ativan and I calmed down.

Every day, when my mother walks me into school, she stops for a minute and says hello to the guards. She looks them in the eye and smiles at them and reminds me to, also. Troy is African-American, like my favorite person Martin Luther King. Ray is from Ethiopia and eats his lunch with a pancake which is also a plate. Gus is Latino and has a wife and a new baby named Ariela. None of them are Jewish. On *Purim*, my mother brings them *hamantashen*. Before 9/11, there weren't any guards and they used to keep the door open with a wooden wedge and when my mom would drop me off and pick me up she would steal the wedge and put it in her purse so that the door would close tight behind her. That's what you call situational ethics, like a white lie, like a bad thing you do for a reason that's good. When I grow up I want to be a judge or a lawyer. I'm a Democrat. The first law I will make is that food is free.

Someone else who is not Jewish that I like is the Dalai Lama. There is a book about him in the library at school. When he was three, monks came to his farm and showed him things belonging to the Dalai Lama before him and he kept taking them and saying "Mine, mine." That's how they knew it was really him. Before they knew, when he was just a baby, he would play a game where he would pack a suitcase like he was going on a long journey. And before that he would gently gather eggs from the hen house with his mother, never dropping them even though his hands were still very small. You can find out more about him at www.dalailama.com. He has a blog, and in it he wrote that most everyone needs more affection and compassion and that not having enough of that is why many people are depressed. He says that if we have sympathy for the suffering of others, we will help remove their pain, and our own serenity and inner strength will increase. These aren't my words, they are actually his, and I cut and pasted them from his site. At the end of his blog he always says, "Do you understand?" which I think is very nice and patient and it makes you feel like he is talking straight to you. I'm not allowed on the computer at home, but I can use the one in the media lab at school. On Thursdays, after school, I go to yoga on Larchmont with my mom and do "downward dog" and "child's pose." Afterward, Mom gets a dry nonfat caf and I get Pinkberry. When they first took the Dalai Lama from his home and he had to sleep all alone, he would make friends with the mice so he wouldn't feel scared.

My favorite portion is the binding of Isaac. It is easy to imagine and very dramatic. G-d tells Jacob… I write G-d with a dash in case you decide to throw this paper away. You're not supposed to say G-d's actual name. There are lots of code names for G-d where you put the letter next to the letter in the Hebrew alphabet in the place of the letter you want. Like in the song Kol Dodi you can switch the letters that are Daled for the next letter in the Hebrew alphabet, which is Hey, and you get the name of G-d. But if you do that, don't say it out loud, because you're not supposed to. The same way you are not supposed to look straight at the sun in an eclipse, so instead you hold a piece of white cardboard out and look at the reflection of the eclipse. That is the best way to say G-d's name, by saying it at an angle, like a code you could read if you held up something in the mirror.

So G dash D says to Abraham that he has to take his son and make a sacrifice of him. It is a test. Abraham binds Isaac and raises a knife to him. He holds it up in the air and there is a lot of suspense. Just then, an angel comes and tells Abraham to stop. The whole time Isaac's eyes are big as saucers, like anime, because he has so much trust for his father. I think that Abraham knew that G-d would interrupt him the whole time. I think Abraham knew it was a test and he was just going along with it. That's how sure he was about G-d. At that very instant, there is a rustling in the brush, and there is a ram tangled in the thicket, and Abraham sacrifices the ram instead, which made me very sad when I heard it. This is one of the reasons I am a vegetarian. My favorite thing is when my father takes me to Joshua Tree and we lie on our backs on a boulder and look up at stars.

I am not always sure about G-d. Sometimes I worry that he is made up by people. There is a boy in my school and he cannot speak. It is hard for him even to look at another person. When I tell you this I feel like crying. He makes a singing sound, like a song you might make up if you had to wait a long time or if you were trying to make yourself calm when you couldn't sleep. The song sounds like when we come into the sanctuary on Yom Kippur, like the sounds of all the people praying to themselves. He has a person who is with him all the time and sometimes when he sees you in the hall, he touches the side of your face and you try to hold very still so that he can. Without talking you know that he is kind. His name is Tal, which is the Hebrew word for dew. And he is like that, like a secret drop of water in the cup of a leaf. The reason I am not sure about G-d is that there have always been wars. Los Alamos, New Mexico has the highest mean IQ of any city in the country. That is because the atom bomb was invented there and those are the kids and grandchildren of the scientists who made the bomb. The person who came up with the bomb was Oppenheimer. He was a non-practicing Jew. After he finished making the atomic bomb he said "I am become death." Every person matters, like Rosa Parks, and the man who stepped in front of the tank in Tiananmen Square, and my brother Natan, and Tal, and also J. Robert Oppenheimer. His wife was named Kitty. There is a lot about him on Wikipedia, but some of it you should not read, because it is very upsetting.

Sometimes when I have a disturbing image that will not go away, I climb into the letters of the *Sh'ma*. The *Sh'ma* is the supreme watchword of our faith. That is what the Rabbi says before we say it. Everyone stands up and you cover your eyes with your hand. These are the words: *Sh'ma Yisroel Adonai Elohenu Adonai Echad*. Here is what they mean: Hear O' Israel the Lord is our G-d the Lord is one. This is what I do. When I close my eyes, I picture the letters of the words. The first Hebrew letter is *shin*, which looks like a sailboat with three sails. In my mind the letter is red, which comes from having synesthesia, which means that your senses cross over each other so that numbers have colors and you can taste sound. When the Jews received the Torah at Mt. Sinai, they had synestheia too, because they saw voices. In my mind, the red sailboat *shin* is tall. I am little when I stand next to it, and I have to reach up to climb it, but I can do it. I sit in the first curve of it and look up at the sail. When I feel like it, I move on to the *mem*, which actually looks like a little cave or a shelter. I sit inside it and go into *Anajali Mudra* pose, which I learned from Isis at Larchmont Yoga. After *mem* is *ayin* and *yud* and so on 'til the end. My very favorite letter is *lamed* which looks like a horse that you ride with your hands around its neck. Sometimes, when *tefillah* is over, the teacher leans over and gives my shoulder a shake to get my attention. Once she had to call my name three times. Levi, Levi, Levi.

In P.E. one day, we had to stand on one foot like Hillel. Here is the story. Someone wants to convert to Judaism and he is not that serious, he is kind of a troublemaker really. He is only saying it to make trouble. He first goes to Shamai and says, "Teach me everything I need to know about Judaism while you stand on one foot." So Shamai chases him away with a stick that he was using to measure something. Next, he goes to Hillel, and Hillel takes him up on it and says, "What is hateful to you, do not do unto thy fellow." Then he says, "Now go and study." I like the feeling of that story. It is like another story where the Pope sends a message to Da Vinci and asks for a sample of work for a commission (hint: it is for the Sistine Chapel, so you know already that it works out.) Da Vinci doesn't want to bother, but the Pope sends message after message like a stalker. Finally, Da Vinci says enough already, and he draws a circle by hand on a piece of paper. That's how he gets the job. Because drawing a perfect circle on a piece of paper is practically impossible, but Da Vinci can do it. I like that both stories have the most simple answer ever. If everyone did A: Treated others the way they would want to be treated, then B: The world would be a perfect circle. It is like a very orderly math equation.

If I told you all the terrible things people have done to each other you would not go out of your house. You would cover your head with your hands and you would pray even if you weren't sure about G-d. If, in the morning, I see the *New York Times* and the *Los Angeles Times* on the table where my dad has his coffee, if I see upside down that a very shocking and terrible thing has happened to a gay person, or to students at a school, or in Darfur or in a library to a little boy while his mother was nearby, I have to save it up like holding a sip of air until I let it out during *tefillah* at school. I pray it out and send it as fast as I can to G-d like smoke up a chimney. I pour the bad feelings into the letters, as if they are little cups, and I sing them out and up. When they open the ark, it is like my chest opening, like a book opening on your lap, like the beginning of a story and you know that you will start to feel better soon. The Torah scrolls are like four kings with velvet covers and crowns. The case they are in is white, white marble and has lions to protect it. Once, they rolled the whole scroll down the long aisle of the sanctuary and all of the children from the Day School stood on either side and very delicately held it up. It was as long as a road. A scribe came to visit us, and used a quill to make the letters. No one took a single breath as he dipped the white quill into the wet black ink and made an *aleph*. The top of the letter started to dry even before he had finished the bottom. It is like when a mother kisses you on the head and for a minute, your skin feels wet and then it doesn't. If a scribe makes a mistake on a scroll, they entirely have to bury it.

There are some people in each generation who protect us. There are thirty-six of them and they are called *Lamed Vovniks*. The letters in Hebrew also stand for numbers and *lamed* stands for thirty and *vav* stands for six. Their prayers go very swiftly up to G-d because they are entirely righteous. You can never know who they are. They could be the person who you would least expect. In the story they read us at school, they are usually a peddler or a shoemaker. If they are a shoemaker, they forget to take your money. They are the people that are in the world but you don't notice them. You are sure they will be there, like the sun or the sky, like grass. If there are not thirty-six, then the world will be in peril. Usually there is something that everyone is praying for as hard as they can. Almost always a very wealthy person sits up at the front of the temple and everyone is surprised that it doesn't work. Then a simple quiet person comes and the skies open up, and the rain comes, and everything is all right. The next day, the person is gone. The shop where the shoemaker was is wide open and he is missing. Everyone goes and collects their shoes and walks around in circles in their new soles going "Who knew?"

I think that when you die, it is the same as before you were born. I think that heaven is the feeling you have when the room is sunny and you are awake but your eyes are not open. I think that my brother is in heaven. Even though he is older than I am, he is a baby. I think that if G-d called him back just at the last second, he must have had a very gentle heart. That if he were here, and knew what I knew, the things I have told you, that his heart would be broken, and that he would have walked around from person to person with his hand out, like waiting for a coin, asking people to help him repair the world. Or that he would have prayed with so much sadness that the sanctuary would have filled with his tears and the chairs and even the Torahs would have been lost in the torrent. He was all love and no bone and his lungs were never even filled with air. It was like two strong angels took him by each arm and rushed him back to heaven. And he only had a minute to look behind him and see my mother holding the baby he was. And he played at the feet of G-d's throne, and that is where he met me and said, "I'll stay here—you go," and the feeling I have in my chest when my heart pounds and my arms feel empty is from the falling, falling down to earth.

The False Bride

OUTSIDE OF SIMON'S OFFICE, the hum of angels' wings moved the air like an evening breeze. The pair, one young and one old—ageless really—but one wise, one unknowing, innocent, rested on the air and waited. The wise one, we will call Gabriel, not because that is his name—angels are nameless, but instead are called by a chord of music, bright and blaring, rich and resonant, depending. But for you gentle reader, you can use that to summon him. The other we will call Micha. Gabriel and Micha rested on the air outside and above Simon's office, which was actually a converted garage and would have to be restored if he ever sold the house. Gabriel, bored of waiting, asked Micha what he had. Micha reached from under his wing and brought forth a story that would break the heart of the reader. It played out in the air between them—something like a hologram, but with *gidicht*—Yiddish for "substance." The characters in the story were not ephemeral, but utterly real, and gasped the air they were brought into like an infant born. Micha presented the beautiful story to Gabriel. "It is a love story," he began.

"Of course, a love story. What else would it be?" Gabriel shifted into the soft air and settled in more comfortably.

In the house there is a beautiful girl sweeping. She is singing to herself and crying. Micha almost forgets himself and moves to reassure her, but he cannot, because unlike in the world, he has no influence here; he can not change the shape of her life, he can only watch it unfold. The sound of her sweeping echoes her loneliness and sounds like the brooms on the stone steps of Jerusalem in the Old City at sunrise. A man enters the room, and it can only be the girl's father. He is poor that is certain, and in the brief moment that the door is ajar, on the air drifts the smell of a bereft soup—the earth of the potato that can only wish to be more, the fleeting sweetness of the carrot. The father crosses to the girl and, standing before her, sets aside her broom and lifts her chin. Her eyes remain cast down. "*Fegele*," he calls her, "Little Bird, it is the day of your sister's wedding."

"Acch," cries Gabriel; he can see where this is going. "The sister will marry the one she loves, what is new under the sun? Nothing."

"Wait," says Micha, pleased to have bested his mentor. "That much is true, but this is also true."

The girl dries her eyes and curtsies in her worn dress to her father, who leaves the room. The house disappears behind her as she climbs the stairs to her room in the attic. She draws her dress over her head, and we see that she is in fact a little bird—the plane of her back like the snowy pages of an unwritten book. She takes the pillow from the bed, draws it to her chest and sobs silently. At that moment, her older sister enters, and we see that while one is graceful and the other plain, one cream and the other water, they are in their bodies sisters. Side by side, they undress in the weak light of the candle—they could be twins. The wedding dress hangs on the closed door and as they stand, each in her thin cotton slip, the bride does the most extraordinary thing; she takes her sister's hands in hers and kisses her tears away. She turns, and taking the wedding dress from the door, slips it over the head of her younger sister. In this moment, they conspire to deceive the con-gregation. Like Leah and Rachel in reverse, the older, less-extraordinary sister makes a gift of the groom. The younger sister makes a show of resisting, but the elder insists. She places and lowers the veil on the false bride, then crawls under the down covers of the bed and wraps a shawl around her own face. The false bride kisses her sister and races downstairs to her wedding.

"Such is the gift of love," muses Micha. Gabriel huffs.

"But the story is not over," Micha reveals with pleasure, as if unfurl-ing the tapestry of a rich silken carpet.

From under his wing he produced a shimmering silken *chuppah*, embroidered by the steady hand of both daughters as they waited to be married off—the edges decorated with split pomegranates, the jeweled seeds sparkling and edged with golden thread. The angel sprays the sky with stars and the small klezmer musicians play their aching clarinet. And, disguised by the veil, the false bride is married to her beloved. He paces around her seven times and shatters with force the cup they have both sipped from. As the newlyweds drive off in their carriage, a fallen star is reflected in the window where the unselfish older sister watches the pair ride off.

Micha disperses the scene with a puff of air and we enter instead the bridal chamber. The bride, shy of her deception, is concealed by the darkness and still wearing the veil as her husband makes love to her, kisses every inch of her body, tasting her, his hands learning her at once. She arcs and hears a startling sound escape her mouth, astounded at her own freedom and passion. She knows she will do anything for him. He collapses beside her, spent. She surprises herself, her own body new to this, ready again. She clings to him. He draws himself away, leaving her aching, her skin cool where he had warmed her. "I cannot love you," he tells her. "I love someone else." She is about to reveal herself, when he begins to extol her own virtues. It is impossible to resist the compliment, so she leans out of the moonlight as he speaks. He tells her that she is water and that her sister is cream. That she is only bone and her sister is fire. He enumerates each of her qualities, and with distilled bitterness, tells her what her sister is not. She grows cold and draws the thin sheet around her, astounded and distressed at what he has said to her beloved sister on her wedding night. The light of the moon casts across his pale skin and she sees that he is nothing—his cruelty to her dear sister unprovoked and selfish. When she reveals herself to him, she draws up the sheet and sees that it is bloodstained. And though his apologies are desperate and earnest, she is deaf to them.

Micha then gathers the story like jewels in a satchel and resists the temptation to look directly at Gabriel, whom he sees is dabbing his eyes and sniffing quietly. "Where is he?" Gabriel barks. "Where is

Simon? Do we have all day?" Micha, though young, is wise enough to conceal his pleasure. It was a good story. He thought as much when he had selected it from the trove of words and images that are stored at the entry of the world to come. He felt reassured that he had not made the rookie mistake of selecting a story with a lesson—like an eager young rabbi who loses the string of his story, like a boy who leaves *cheder*, and in his daydreams, loses his way.

Gabriel and Micha yet waited. Micha saw that it was spring, that the lilac, which all the while had been a bony stick, had sprouted leaves of intention; that daily, hourly it claimed its place. It was nearly Purim, when the ecstatic yelling and stomping of Jews celebrated their victory over a villain whose name they would write in chalk on their shoes. A story with all the best elements: a beautiful heroine, a deception, a villain, a revelation, a punishment so elegantly contrived that only the cruel perpetrator could become its victim. On *Erev Purim*, at the close of the *Fast of Esther*, Gabriel and Micha would fly around the world moving toward the west so that the sun would set and set and set and the *megillah* would be unfurled and through the voices of men and women tell the story that would not resolve till morning. But today they continued to linger, awaiting the writer, due to arrive, who was so late they wondered if he too was first encircling the world. Only Gabriel had begun to worry, but he saw that the young angel was so pure in his mission, so eager, that he did not flag, that Gabriel did not betray his concern, and instead made idle conversation.

"Do you know the story about Rabbi Hillel?" Gabriel tested, "the one where he lay on the roof of the *cheder* looking through the skylight?" Micha lifted his head from the leaves he was watching. This is how young he is, thinks Gabriel, he can wonder at leaves without thinking of death. Micha gives Gabriel his full attention. "What angel does not know that story? So great was his love for Torah that he does not know his own comfort, nearly freezing to death. So beautiful, like petals pressed between pages." Gabriel is patient through the retelling. He takes his moment. "The story was almost lost." Micha turns, his eyes widen. "I know, because I was there that day." Micha is rapt and Gabriel cannot deny the pleasure of it. "I was like you, new to it. It was my first delivery," Gabriel continued.

"It was a bitter wind and the fields and streets were an endless expanse of white. You could not see where the snow ended and the sky began, that is how white it was, blinding. My partner, Ishmael, held the story to his bosom like an infant through the relentless weather. I was a pisher, they gave me only the simplest tales to ferry, that I might not drop them and let them spill out like a case of souls. I had to struggle to keep up, though I was the younger, so intrepid was Ishmael, so urgent was the delivery of the story. The writer...." Here Gabriel stops himself, as if he can go no further with the story. Micha nearly topples so far does he lean. The wizened angle draws him closer. "The writer," he continues, like parsing bread to a goose, "the writer got lost in the storm. The story nearly..." And here he need not continue, the fate of an untold story was well known to Micha, who gathered his wing about *The False Bride* with still more care. He could hear the voices of the characters at a distance like the hum of bees.

"The writer, it seems, was hungry. His wife lay in bed, nursing a new son, and for days and days the writer had given his food to them—his wife unaware of her husband's sacrifice. He had assured her that he had more than enough because he did not want the fear of their future to become the world of the baby she carried. When the child was born, he took all that he had and filled the house with food and wood and blankets made of wool, but in the end there was nothing left for him. And as he fed his wife so that she may feed their son, he told her that he had already eaten and could not eat a bite more. In her portion, he put a piece of meat, the broth rich with a bone and its marrow, and he stood over her so that she finished it and wiped the bowl with bread. She leaned her head on the pillow and lay watching her nursing son, and she thanked God for the child and the blessing of their bounty. The writer told his bride and his child that he needed to cut firewood and he went out under the stars and prayed. He wrote when he could in a small shed with a tallow candle. He promised himself that when he had chopped the wood, he would set a warm fire in the stove for his wife and child and return to the shed when she was sleeping. The world was still and silent but for the sound of Ishmael and me where we hovered above the shed and waited for him. When we saw that he had left the house, we rose and readied ourselves, presenting the story like a feast on a silver tray. But instead he turned away from us and went to the woodpile, the smoke from the chimney a thin grey ribbon on the darkening sky. We waited, and the writer raised the axe to split the wood, but the axe flew back heavy in his hands and he could not fell it. But it felled him."

"Ah!" Micha gasped at the telling. Gabriel smiled and Micha righted himself.

"But you know the story, you know that it was written, so why do you worry?" Micha cast his eyes down, but Gabriel spared him. "The writer was exhausted from hunger. And the weight of the axe bore him down. He lay splayed in the snow, his eyes open but sightless, as the stars, first three, then as many as the sons of Abraham, fill the sky above him. He lay this way as the snow began to fall and, as if in a gentle sleep, the snow became a blanket for him." Micha's eyes implored Gabriel to go on. "What can we do? We are only angels? We have only to deliver the story," cautioned Gabriel, "We are not the authors of people's lives." He continued. "When the young mother awakens the room is bitter with cold. She can see her own breath, and the cheeks of the infant feel cool against hers. She leaps from the bed and cries out to her husband. With the infant in her arms, his eyes wide to the world, she runs in her stocking feet out to the yard. She is stopped stark at the dark night, the sky black as the wet ink of the scribe, the only sound her hard heart pounding. She scans the yard and that is when she sees him, the shape of him, beneath the snow. She cries out and runs to the place where he had fallen, the weight of the infant and the slowness of her own movement a shock to her. Even as she bore him in her arms, she had forgotten that she was a mother, still so much a wife. She lay the swaddled child in the snow beside her husband and began to dig with her bare hands to release him."

The sound of Simon's Prius, so nearly silent that he had arrived undetected by the angels at the door of his converted office. He struggled with the key, jiggling it just so— he would have to call a locksmith or not lock it. Well he'd better, there had been a lot of thefts in the neighborhood and even though he saved what he was writing in the ether by emailing it to himself everyday, it would be a huge hassle to replace his laptop—though he liked the look of the one he had seen at the Mac store at the Grove, the one that was so thin you could slip it into an envelope. He gave the door a shove with his hip and felt a sense of relief wash over him as he entered this small, but his, place. He felt the hideous traffic of the 405 receding. He kept his Emmy in here so that it would greet him winged and feminine, years old, but joyful of his return. He had faith in only one thing, that if he arrived in the room every day, something would get written. He turned to shut the door behind him, and as he pressed the door closed he discerned the jasmine on the air, but not the angels who had whisked in with the speed of Elijah sipping from his cup of the Seder table and out again, leaving *The False Bride* behind.

Above Simon's small workspace, Gabriel hastened to return to the gates of heaven, for this was to be his last assignment. Micha followed after him, breathless with the success of his mission, the fragile daughters safe in the hands of the writer. When he had made up the space between them, Micha tugged at Gabriel to finish the story of his first assignment. Gabriel pretended for his own amusement not to know what he wanted. They hovered then, the gates of heaven glistening in the distance, and Gabriel continued. "The father? What became of him? When his bride cleared the snow from his eyes and his nostrils, he saw her and with her help he was able to stand. She carried the child in one hand and led her husband into the house with the other. She put him in her own bed with the infant, and she herself chopped wood and stoked the fire. She sucked out the marrow from the bones and fed it to him like the mother of a bird."

"And then?" Micha could not bear it.

"And then, he was overtaken with fever and by morning he had died."

Micha gasped. "Died?"

"Died and left the son an orphan and the bride a widow."

Gabriel put his hand on the shoulder of the young angel; he knew how he suffered.

"How could he have died?"

"Because it's not a story."

Micha nodded. Of course it was not a story, but the helpless truth. He knew better. His heart ached for the widow and orphan. Together the angels moved up toward heaven and Micha felt the relief of knowing his days would be filled with the work of stories, each as achingly sweet as the lilacs that would bloom in just weeks outside of Simon's office. Micha stopped and turned suddenly to Gabriel. "But the story?"

Gabriel looked at him, pleased as a father. "We gave it to the child. We set it in his cradle and he grew beside it and played with it as other children play with toys. Each day he rose, he saw Hillel search his empty pockets and climb the roof to lay on the skylight and listen to the reading of the Torah."

"…And the snow fell and covered him like a blanket and he nearly froze to death…" Micha continued. "Oh, no" says Gabriel, correcting him. "That was not part of the story we delivered. That was the writer's own invention."

Good

RAFE MENDELSSOHN took the last hot draw of his cigarette and wondered if he was good. He flicked the end of the spent Marlboro and crushed it under his Donald Pliner loafer, rocking his foot back and forth like a dance step, then, bending over in a suit that moved with him, retrieved the useless filter and dropped it into his pocket. Then, like gathering the evidence from a crime scene, he scanned the courtyard of the temple and opened the heavy wooden door, returning back to morning services on the Day of Atonement. In the lobby illuminated by white bulbs to honor the dead, he wondered about his father, who certainly could be dead; he wasn't sure if he'd be called or not. He didn't want to think about it. He was smiled at aggressively by a red-headed member of the Sisterhood as she pressed a black satin yarmulke into the palm of one of the older congregants who appeared on the High Holidays. The man's snow white hair was combed immaculately, his nails buffed pink. The woman's hairstyle carbon-dated her to be somewhere in her late seventies. Rafe smiled back at her Clooney-style, his head tucked slightly, his eye cast up. She was slayed by him. Wearing the white rose corsage that identified her as an usher, she came from behind the table that offered hearing devices, and like his prom date, moved to his side and tucked her arm into his. She guided him to the side door, where his entrance would be the least disruptive. They were silent on tiptoe and she ducked away demurely as he slid into the sanctuary like a teenager home after curfew.

The rabbis, who like so many people in LA looked like they played themselves on TV, were dressed in white for the holiday, white unadorned and pure, meant to suggest the kittle you are buried in; you stood before your maker, ready to die, in case things didn't go your way. Rafe didn't own a white suit, didn't want to own one, and felt more at ease in his own clothes, his leather belt and shoes. In his hometown in New Jersey, the men wore sneakers to temple on Yom Kippur. He remembered them drinking schnapps around a table at the break-fast, his own father conspicuously absent, his ticket paid for begrudgingly by the congregation. He wondered for a moment if his father went to temple. He had no idea. He would be old now, he realized, his hair white. The last time he saw him, over ten years ago, he had already started to look like Phil Donahue.

Rafe scanned the congregation for Ayelet Halpern, the pretty wife who he knew would be alone that day, her unconverted husband only willing to come as near to the temple as the carpool lane. He liked the way she smelled. The seat beside her was open, not accidentally, and he made his way for it, slipping into her row and grabbing a prayer book from the back of the seat in one move. Ayelet wore a slim sheath, her hair like the black coffee he had this morning to take the edge off his fasting. Her bare shoulder pressed against his sleeve as she leaned back to whisper to him and that was the best part—the color commentary she offered on the service, his breathing her warm skin and hair in plain sight of the congregation, Ayelet not abiding the rule against perfume and smelling something like warm sheets and a sugar cookie.

Rafe sat back in the green velvet seat built like a chair in an older movie theatre. He thought of the movies he didn't see while he felt up Sharona Sussman at the Stanley Warner theatre in Paramus. They tested his movies there now, at the same theatre he would go to with his father on Saturdays, when he would come in from the city in a rental car and let Rafe tool around the parking lot in the back. His father, always willing to be the favorite parent, letting him drive and eat cheeseburgers, taking him at nine to the opening of Barbarella where he saw, under the lens of her spacesuit, a single perfect nipple, the one he imagined when he kneaded the newly ripe apricot that was Sharona Sussman's breast.

Rafe crossed his legs and opened the prayer book across his knee. It was a new modernized edition, written by the rabbi, with annotated English text on the sides to occupy a distracted congregation. Rafe preferred the heavily weighted text of his youth—the Hebrew that was chanted around him in the men's section by the resonant voices of men who did not for the most part take an interest in him as his mother had hoped. Still, he was reassured by the fact of them and the idea of who he might become. Rafe was relegated at home to the women's section, living with his mother and sister, the bathroom closet always stocked like a hospital with Kotex and tampons, the sink ornamented with black cake eyeliner and bobby pins. In the Orthodox temple of his youth, he was, if nothing else, briefly relieved of that, smelling instead the soapy clean smell of men, the leather of the straps on the tefillin. Barneys, he had to admit, smelled just the same way and, when he left Greengrass after his lox, eggs, and onions for the hidden men's department on the fifth floor, he felt happily sequestered, at home.

"Do you forgive me?" Ayelet leaned back and whispered. She flirted ruthlessly and then, didn't, leaving him feeling as if he had imagined it. It was all the better, it made him crazy. Throughout the service she made excuses to cross her legs, which were sheathed in stockings, something women never wore in LA outside of role-play. When they were young, walking home from temple, Rafe's sister would torment him. Ariel would punch him hard in the arm, as he was forbidden to hit her back. " Do you forgive me?" she would say, "Do you forgive me?" She would punch him again and then, repeating the question once more, "Do you forgive me?" she would punch him a third time. His sister exploiting the elegant condition of forgiveness in Judaism, that if you have asked to be forgiven by someone three times and they have denied you, the sin is and its burden becomes theirs.

Ayelet rocked the heel of her pump, the shoe held on barely by her pointed toe. Women, and what they wanted and what they hated and were afraid of and required and found charming, was what Rafe knew.

Women were his best thing. That he was handsome made it that much easier to repair to them. To the narrow beds of their dorm rooms, to their sleeping bags, to the fold-out sofas of their parents' den, one girl giving him head while driving from New York to Boston, her long hair in waves across his thighs, her head petted by his free hand, the other on the wheel, his eyes trained on the white dashes that divided the road. "I don't know," he whispered back. Rafe caught the eye of Rabbi Beth as she sat in the high chair on the back of the *bima*. He was busted and he straightened up in his seat, looked at the row ahead of him for the page. 127. The *V'ahavta*. The truth was he loved to pray. He loved the low thunder of it in the large room. He didn't actually attend to each word; in fact, despite having gone to an Orthodox yeshiva almost through high school, he didn't know the meaning of each and every word. But that didn't matter to him. When he joined his voice with the others it was like stepping skillfully onto a train that was already moving. Taking hold and pulling himself up, relieved, proud even, to have made the leap with such surety. Secure in his footing, he would let the words carry him. The new edition of the prayer book was still rife with "Almighty Gods" and "my sovereign, my shield" and although Rafe had long since stopped imagining a father in heaven, he felt relief and power in the words, to believe as a boy in a God with an outstretched arm, a God who parted seas. A God he had prayed to for the return of his father. While praying, the tunes familiar and reassuring, Rafe took in the beautiful room, the instructive stained glass that illustrated the tribes, the four pillars *Charity, Justice, Repentance,* and *Prayer* like tent poles that held the ceiling sixty feet above. He could attend, if he wished, to the voice of the woman beside him, whose ownership of the melody impressed him, reminded him of Ariel, made him miss her. When he thought of Ariel, Rafe's anger at this father was always redoubled. She was funny and smart and beautiful and volleyed between safe men and hazardous men, sometimes using one to unravel the other. That their father did not see *her* was the greater insult to him. When they were young, Rafe adored her, protected her in the ways that he could. He would be alert to small changes in her appearance and notice them, telling her that he liked her part that way, that a blouse was pretty on her, that she was talented at drawing. When she told him in junior high that the father who drove her home after her babysitting job had grabbed at her breast and pushed his tongue between her teeth, Rafe had woken at three in morning and rode his bike the six miles to slash the tires on the man's Volvo. From the pay phone at the Suburban diner, Rafe called the man's house every day after school for five years, hanging up just as he answered, the tires of his bike throwing off gravel as he rode away. He knew that the man thought he could get away with it, had gotten away with it, because Ariel had no father, that the cool air of risk was about his sister, because they had only a boy to protect them. When right out of college Ariel had been hired to design the book jacket of a collection of stories by Isaac Bashevis Singer, she had called their father to tell him, and Rafe watched her first ebullient and proud and then made small before his eyes. Hanging up the phone, and trying bravely to deflect the injury, Rafe had tucked her whole self into his chest and kissed her head, while she cried briefly into his shirt, but only briefly. Wiping her nose on his sleeve they both laughed. Nothing was more known to them than the absurd persistence of the expectation that next time it would be different; that one of these days he would be their father, as if walking head long into plate glass, righting yourself, and with your head still ringing, walking into plate glass again.

Rabbi Snow asked the congregation to rise and Rafe came to the part of the service he liked the best, an acrostic of sins you may have committed. He didn't know why it was his favorite, but it had always been, making a fist of your hand and pounding your heart with each mention of the A to Z, Aleph through Tav of sins. The heart, the place where sin harbors. The language of the prayer collective. The sins that *we* have committed. The tense, past perfect. *Ashamnu*, we have been guilty. Rafe tripped over the same ones year after year, *Lashon Hara*, gossip, he tried but couldn't help it. He loved to be around women and that was the coin of their realm, loving less the party than the debriefing afterward. And of course the sin of coveting which he did even now, the curve of his neighbor's breast the edge of the earth as it disappeared into her dress lovely at the angle he held. "Don't go mistaking heaven for the home across the road," he reminded himself, a commandment of Bob Dylan, but still Rafe tried to observe it. Rafe's eyes caught and lingered on the words of the prayer *bimutz ha lev*—the hardening of our heart and even reading the words brought a tightness to his chest.

The truth is he tried to be good. He was honest in his work, attentive and respectful to everyone in his employ. This he learned from his mother who modeled it aggressively, giving courtesy to everyone as if they were a secret king. He paid them fairly and on time, aware of the yearning and shame that came from having to ask, as his mother had had to so that they might attend the Day School and have a seat on the holidays. It was his shame only, his mother bearing it instead with something that felt more like pride at who he was and what he could be, that it was she who was doing them a favor. It was no effort to honor his mother. Every year from vow to vow, all conduct could be improved, corrected, all but one, the honoring of father.

Rabbi Snow's sermon, Rafe knew, would culminate with a plea for money. Rafe was happy to write the check, to fold down the tab on the request for Israel Bonds. Every year he subsidized a child in the Day School and he felt the same way he had replacing the roof on his mother's house when he was only twenty-five, that he was doing the right thing. It gave him a deep sense of satisfaction. When the Social Action committee came to him and asked for twenty thousand dollars, he wrote a check for thirty. On Big Sunday, he got everyone in his office to plant a garden and repaint a school in East LA. But he had no interest in forgiving his father. Rafe didn't love his father, didn't like him, had no pity for him that he could locate, which made him suspect that he must still hate him, not with the recklessness he felt as a boy when he had left their family, but with the distilled confidence of a man. The sin, he knew, was becoming his.

To even think of forgiving his father made Rafe shift in his seat, his body so uncomfortable with the impossible-to-solve equation. Over his shoulder, Rafe watched as the white haired man he had seen in the lobby, slowly returned to his seat. Each time Rafe turned back, the man seemed to have advanced not at all as if he and the rabbi were playing a protracted game of "red light green light." It made Rafe weary even to explain to himself his reluctance to forgive. Not to others—a successful man is able to justify himself easily in the world, as if all choices that lead to this moment were the right ones. But to himself, to God, he wrestled with it, resented his father even more for leaving him this dilemma. His father was a least as old as the man who moved so slowly and used the back of each wooden bench as a rest in his undetectable progress. Rafe felt almost like a bully to harbor anger toward a now elderly man. But the harm he suffered at his father's hand was in all of Rafe, and he had caused this harm, without raising a hand to him.

Rafe remembered when he was twelve, his father rented a car and collected him and Ariel and drove him to his home in Brooklyn Heights and there, like in a perverse children's story, Rafe and his sister met the doppelgangers that were his father's new family. A boy and a girl, nearly identical in their ages, and, in the kitchen setting the table with the very same china pattern of a house in snow that his mother used at home, was a woman that was a lesser version of his mother. The house in this magical land was in perfect repair; each child had their own room and a closet full of new clothes. Rafe knew that if he stepped into the wardrobe and through time and space to his own life, he would feel the edge of fear that defined their days, on the samovar, the insult to the injury, rested a check for seventeen dollars. Seventeen dollars was not enough for anything, not a whole pair of jeans, not the cost of groceries for the family his father had so easily left. Seventeen dollars was only enough to keep the state from putting Rafe's absent father in arrears. Rafe's mother would sit at the same table where they had Shabbat and would wonder aloud if it were more useful to make from the check paper dolls and how she might parse it between the bills for heat and tuition. Rafe learning from his father that a parent may unchoose you, may make less of you, may make you vanish altogether. Years later, at a screening of his own film, Rafe was introduced to a man who he knew had worked with his father. Rafe identified himself as Abe Mendelssohn's son, only to be told "You must be Aaron." The fact of them, Rafe and his sister, a reluctant truth that his father was able, in years that followed, to barely recall, misremember, and eventually believe himself had never existed. His father's sleep, Rafe was sure, had

been untroubled, but for the knocking and footfall of the family he had
hidden from himself behind the wallboards and under the floors.

Rafe wondered if his father prayed. He wondered if he too was
seated now in a temple, a part of a community, greeted by people who
liked him. Rafe remembered his father, handsome and charming, all
women in his company bending toward him like flowers yearning toward a sun; every waitress and store clerk, the woman at the toll booth
on the George Washington Bridge, a smile lingering on her face as a
young Rafe tossed the coins into the just out of reach basket. Yes, Rafe
concluded, he would be a beloved member of his congregation, his
wife beside him and the better best children on either side. Rafe struggled, wishing to be man enough to release his anger, but he could not
remember himself without it. It was not different now than it was then,
not after a thousand dutiful hours in therapy trying to reshape it, hon-
ing it instead. He is still young, without power, and he sees early and
plainly that the world is a danger to his sister, to his mother, and he is
afraid for them and he can do nothing, very little. A teenager, he lies
on his bed with his eyes open and knows on the same world is a father
that was meant to be theirs, his, and that his father just across the
bridge is thisclose, but in the end as good as dead. Not as good as, because if he were dead, the congregation would have encircled them,
put their collective strength behind them and lifted him up. But his
father was not dead, he was proximate and able, in a wrestling that
seemed not at all hard, to live without them. A tension in his chest reminded him that his father might die before he could come to forgiveness. He tried to plan for the possibility and tested himself, tried to
discern love or courage, but again he found in himself only a tightening
of his limbs, drawing himself in, the feeling of turning in a small space.

Ayelet touched Rafe's sleeve and even without his attention, his
skin was charged by it. Her head cast down, he saw that she had been
crying, her own prayer transporting her to a place of loss. She gathered
herself, smiled and rose to slip past him, something he knew she
would do carelessly in a kind of deliciously slow motion. Rafe moved
back to make way for her, and stepping into the aisle was face to face

with the old man he had been watching, who had only just reached the back of their chair, when looking at Rafe as if he were searching, he clutched his chest and drew a raspy chain of air for the last time, and this is how Rafe came to be holding him as he fell, a gasp of perfect unison drawn by the congregation as two dozen doctors of assorted specialties looked on.

Ayelet dropped to her knees and started compressions and Rafe, as if they did this all the time, as if this were their occupation, placed his mouth over the mouth of the man who had fallen. Rafe was shocked at the first push of air into the man's lungs, how like a bellows it was, how mechanical. Rafe heard a swoon, which he concluded, must be the wife of the man fainting and another ripple of activity, a sisterhood of women attending to her. He heard counting and as he rocked his head to the side to listen for air escaping the man's mouth. Rafe observed Ayelet in her dress and heels, her slender arms locked, pressing on the man's chest, who would have rallied if only he had known. They made quick eye contact and Ayelet counted more loudly as if conducting the congregants around them who counted in unison, "2, 3, 4, 5," Rafe saw that the man's ears and lips were turning blue, and reacting, forced the air into his lungs with more intention. He was surprised how demanding the exercise was and made himself focus, the muscles in his upper thighs hungry for oxygen, smarting like a runner. At a distance Rafe heard the siren pealing through the air. He drew in a breath, and drawing up the man's chin, pushed the breath harder. Ayelet was herself breathing hard with the effort. Her head made a quick turn as the doors to the sanctuary slammed open as the paramedics made their way. "Forgive him," Ayelet said, to Rafe, who regarded her with alarm. "He might die," she insisted, tears forming in the wells of her eyes. "Forgive him." Rafe's own chest tightened: he persisted in his breathing and tried to shape the words to whisper into the ear of this man who lay before him, now blue now pink, a lingering warmth still about him, and tried to form the words and they were trapped in his body. A flood of anger made his eyes sting and, his muscles strengthening so that pushing Ayelet aside, it was he who pressed his fists onto the old man's chest in a way that nearly alarmed the arriving paramedics, who overheard the temple member who was administering CPR say, "Live, you son of a bitch," and, breathing into his lungs, restoring his sinus rhythm, "Don't you dare fucking die."

Beth Beth

RABBI BETH ROSEN was a perfect size two. She had ideal Semitic features—olive skin and deep, brown, almond shaped eyes. Her nose was narrow and even, in a way that made her beauty seem less frivolous. She had appeared on *Grey's Anatomy* in the role of a rabbi giving a blessing over a girl who had refused a porcine heart valve and had opted for beef instead; the cow, having been slaughtered swiftly with a blade sharp enough to split a hair and drained of its blood, before becoming part of the girl in the episode. Rabbi Rosen already had her SAG card from her appearance on *Six Feet Under*, where she appeared in the role of a female rabbi. In another time she might have been the girl at the well.

The desk in front of her was littered with messages of emerging grief. She was to officiate today over a funeral for a man whose wedding she had conducted when he was married to his *beshert* less than a month before. He had died on the table at Cedars during what was meant to be, while not routine, certainly not fatal surgery. The husband had been adopted and there had been only sketchy medical history that had not revealed a clotting issue that caused him to rapidly, almost stealthily, die on the table. Rabbi Beth had gotten a call from Rabbi Meier, the chaplain who was in Cleveland on a book tour and, instead of driving east to the Grove for a movie, she drove west to the hospital. The *kallah*, his bride, had been sitting in the waiting area when Beth arrived, her fingers pressed to her mouth as if she had burned them; she had not moved or spoken since the doctor had given her the news. She was an *onen*, new to her grief, in the first twenty-four hours when a person is not meant to be consoled, but must be allowed to learn the keen truth of their loss. Rabbi Beth sat beside her. The woman, whose eyes were yet dry from her shock, was not young. She had married at thirty-six to this man with whom she intended to begin their belated family. The newlywed couple had been to Cedars four times this month to ready her body for in-vitro. Rabbi Beth had not eaten breakfast this morning and thought that meant she would not throw up, but she did, deftly, almost between thoughts, into the wastebasket under her desk.

She rinsed her mouth in the sink of the Day School restroom and thought the smell of cleanser would cause her to throw up again; she fought back the feeling by imagining herself biting into a lemon the way that her sister-in-law had recommended. She wiped her mouth with the back of her hand and crossed the hall to the office of the senior rabbi at least three weeks before she thought she would have to. She had dressed herself in clever outfits from Lost and Found on Ivar that hung loosely below the bust. She thought she could protect the *nefesh* by keeping the news to herself, but her secret wasn't safe.

Rabbi Beth hung at the doorway, gripping the back of the guest chair like the rail of a ship while Rabbi Snow clasped the hands of the married TV producers who were building the new facility. Rabbi Stu Snow was fifty-one to Beth's thirty-one, but looked as young as she did, boyish in a way that made him trustworthy, so that when he encouraged it, you could accept hope. His wife, Debra, had served on the committee to hire Beth, and Beth resembled her, what Debra had looked like when, as a young law student spending her semester at Bar Ilan, she met her future husband the rabbinical student, who, while waiting for his proposal, she had called "Rabbi Nu?" Beth liked Debra, found her edgier and a bit more worldly than Stu, whose semester in Tel Aviv represented his only sojourn outside of Southern California. Debra, now a federal prosecutor, spent very little time at the Temple and appeared only on major holidays to stand before the congregation blessing the candles with her twin sons, Jake and Sam.

Rabbis Beth and Snow exchanged a glance over the shoulders of the female producer who had created the show—the look married couples on TV exchange when they mean "meet me in the kitchen." The show's creator turned and greeted Rabbi Beth on her way out. Her departure always caused Beth to unconsciously hum the theme song to her show, which had been composed by the husband; Beth had to bite her tongue to keep from doing it. She watched them as they walked down the hall together and Beth wondered if having a show in syndication was enough to make people happy. The temple, she knew, was referred to in the community as Temple Beth Showrunner; it was through the many writers and producers who were members of the congregation that Rabbi Beth had found her unlikely second calling. Rabbi Snow had returned to his seat behind his desk, which sat rakishly at a diagonal in his office. He had taken out a yellow pad to write the first draft of his sermon. He raised a finger to indicate that he needed to get down a quick note. "Can you take the Solomon funeral today?" Beth said, "It's at four." She tried to sound casual and thought that after all she might be able to postpone telling him a few more weeks. "I can do the Steiner mikvah for you." Alison Steiner had recently come out as a lesbian and her adult children meant to mark the transition with an immersion. "Sure," Rabbi Snow said, and finished up his message. Rabbi Beth's shoulders lowered; she hadn't realized how much she had not wanted to tell him. She slowed her steps to make her exit appear relaxed. Rabbi Snow stood up and took his sweater off the back of his chair. Rabbi Beth was about to clear the threshold of his office when she was assaulted by the smell of fresh coffee in the outer room. Once pleasant to her, now the smell filled the back of her throat like viscous, hot tar. It made her gag and her eyes water. She tried to make the three steps across the hall to her own office. "Oh wait," Rabbi Snow called after her, "I've got Jake's teacher's conference today." Rabbi Beth threw up into her own hand.

When Rabbi Snow left her office, Beth remained half-seated on the sill of her window. She pressed her forehead to the cool glass with her eyes closed and replayed the scene of Stu receiving the news. Marilyn, who had brewed the offending coffee, had appeared with a wet paper towel—the rough, gray kind that came folded from the machine in the kids' restroom. The smell of the wet pulp caused her throat to lurch. Beth accepted the towel and used it to pat her forehead holding her breath, then returned it, as if gratefully, to the rabbis' shared secretary. Marilyn gave her a sly smile that threatened a baby shower with a card signed by everyone and surprise gifts of "What to Expect When You're Expecting" tucked onto her swivel chair. Beth was relieved that she would be able to tell Marilyn that it was a Jewish tradition not to buy gifts for the baby before it was born. It was not a tradition, more of a superstition really, but Beth felt it was a small sin to deceive her, not like the congregant who told her non-Jewish husband that the birth of a son required pearls. In Beth's office, Rabbi Snow had stepped forward to congratulate her. "*Mazel Tov!*," he said, Beth thought, a bit too loudly. She had read something else on his face before he composed himself and delivered the blessing—he had kissed her on her still damp forehead like a girl—disappointment. In his look she imagined that he reconsidered the wisdom of hiring a young woman, as if she were not a spiritual leader, but was instead a firefighter who had sued her way into department and would be of little use now, unable to climb ladders or hoist a hose. Beth turned her face, so that her cheek now pressed against the glass.

There were no women on the *bima* when Beth grew up. Beth had not even heard of the heroic Hannah Senesh until she was in college; as a girl in Day School she had had to content herself with Miriam's quiet role in saving her brother Moses, her wisdom in bringing timbrels out of Egypt. It was Beth's father who was the rabbi at their conservative synagogue in Philadelphia. While her father delivered the sermon on the *bima*, Beth's mother would prepare the *kiddish* with the other mothers in the Sisterhood, pouring the wine into the tiny white cups that covered the table at the back of the sanctuary as she delivered her own whispered sermon to the other women about a *simcha* or a *shandeh*. The *rebbetzin* embarked on missions that fell outside the purview of Beth's father, once driving to the house of Mrs. Wise, the most beautiful teacher in the Day School—Beth's mother making false starts, but not explaining the purpose of their visit; Beth, holding the *kugel* on her lap, still warm through the dishtowel and her tights. At the house, Beth set the Pyrex dish onto the dining room table and held the book her mother had instructed her to bring open on her lap, but kept her eyes on her mother, who sat beside the young woman, who seemed tired and small. Beth's mother, quiet and as firm as a judge, spoke not at all, but the woman seemed to listen to her, as if following instructions— first dropping her shoulders, then sobbing and in turn drying her eyes and drawing herself up. They had stayed late in the day till the room had darkened, Beth's mother drawing a blanket around Mrs. Wise atop the still-made bed and kissing the teacher on her head. On the drive home, her mother retold Beth the story of Job whose three friends, seeing that his pain was great, sat with him for seven days and said not a word. Giving proof to what Beth suspected that Mrs. Wise had suffered a terrible unnamed loss. Reaching across, Beth's mother pressed Beth's arm through her sleeve, said, "You're a good girl," then, returning her hand to two o'clock on the steering wheel, she trained her eyes forward and drove them home.

Marilyn cleared her throat, giddy now, pregnant herself with her plans—a banner of linking foil letters, a baby picture of the rabbi herself on the invite, she would hit Smart and Final on the way home from work and pick up paper goods. Rabbi Beth opened her eyes and righted herself. Marilyn was talking, something about an appointment, but Beth was still looking out over the parking lot where a tall handsome husband leaned onto the open car window of a Day School mother who was not his wife. He shifted his body like a teenage boy; the mother pushed her hair back behind her ear, her head cast down, listening. She knew the mother's husband was not Jewish, she had seen him idling his car, picking up their son, Ethan, from religious school.

Dev Brennan stepped into Rabbi Beth's office.

Rabbi Beth abandoned the couple and gave her attention to the man who was taking his seat across from her desk. She reminded herself in the future to move less suddenly. From behind Mr. Brennan, Marilyn miraculously produced a cup of tea and an Osem teething biscuit. She handed it to Beth with a knowing look and Beth forced a smile, hoping that would be enough to make her leave. Beth used the business of setting down the tea to consult her calendar. On her blotter she found it: "Brennan.—Jew by choice." Beth extended her hand to the man, but it went unnoticed by him. "Mr. Brennan," she offered, "Yes," he answered without looking up.

Dev Brennan folded himself into his seat and shifted his position three consecutive times, perplexed, as if it were his first chair. At last he settled on a posture that might work with his legs crossed and one foot hooked behind as if to control it. His hair was black and hung over his blue eyes like the spread wing of a crow. He focused on a point of the floor. Beth mirrored him and looked down at her tea meaning to convey that there was no hurry. "My sister died in the attacks on the Twin Towers," he began, "9/11" he added, as if she might not know which attack, which twin towers. Rabbi Beth lifted her eyes to his, still downcast. "I'm sorry," she said. She had nearly said, "I'm sorry for your loss," like a doctor on ER, but thank God she had caught herself. She wondered when her own words had been replaced by the dialogue of people on television. She ordered herself to inhale and exhale. "When my father was told the news," he continued, his voice singsong like an old Jew telling a joke, "He had a heart attack and died right there on the spot." Rabbi Beth struggled to master her own expression. Mr. Brennan was patting his pockets looking for something and had yet to look up at her. Beth instructed her shoulders to drop. He gave up his search and continued. "My ten year old son, Trevor, has autism." he said without pausing, "and I have an anxiety disorder that makes it impossible to change lanes on the highway." Mr. Brennan retried his pockets in reverse order. He ended his search in a jacket pocket where he found a flattened soft pack of cigarettes. Beth realized it had been a while since she had seen one. The white pack had a target on it and she struggled to remember the brand. At last Mr. Brennan looked up at her, shaking a single cigarette to the surface and drawing it out with his slender fingers. "Can you imagine that? Not being able to change lanes in LA?" "No," she said, she couldn't. Mr. Brennan fished in his breast pocket for matches. Beth pulled the steel drawer of her desk and produced a pack from the narrow tray of pencils and paper clips that been there as long as the desk. She sat waiting expectantly for him to ask if he could smoke. When he didn't, she explained that he couldn't. "I'm sorry," Beth said, vaguely indicating an overhead sprinkler and then, rising said. "Maybe we could go outside."

Rabbi Beth led Dev Brennan out the door of her office. They passed Marilyn's open office door where she sat at her desk on the phone. The secretary lowered her voice as they passed already in the throes of spreading Beth's news like a feather pillow shaken off a rooftop. Rabbi Beth had told the children in the preschool the story of carelessly spoken words just yesterday and watched their worried expressions as they imagined collecting the scattered feathers in their small hands. She had only wanted the *nefesh*, the quietly dividing cells, to be undisturbed. She knew that when thoughts became words, they were at once, more true. That when her pregnancy was described it became more part of the world, less hers. If the child were a boy she would have to, at eight days, deliver him to the *kvatter* who would pass him to the *sandech* for the circumcision and, at thirty days, redeem him a with five shekels or, as they had for her brother, five silver spoons. She had only wanted to protect it. Even the morning when she had held the stick and watched the blue line develop, Beth had not told her husband right away. But instead, she had sat on the edge of the tub and closed her eyes as she hovered in quiet, the way you make your self still, to try and remember a fleeting dream. Some twenty minutes later, she called to her husband and perpetrated the re-enactment. Their marriage was not arranged, but could have easily been, so matched were they in their beauty and promise. He had held her and she had reminded herself to place her trust in him.

Dev Brennan followed Rabbi Beth into the dark cool stairwell that led to the roof. Instinctively they tiptoed to keep their footfall from echoing. The last ascending staircase was shorter and the landing used as storage for earthquake kits—plastic tubs filled with large Ziploc bags inscribed in Sharpie for each child; at the ready, a protein bar and water bottle; in a smaller bag, photos of mom and dad, the family dog, to reassure the child while they waited for their parents to come. At the end of each year that disaster was averted, the photos were returned and the edible contents of the bag were donated to Sova, the food pantry on Beverly across from CBS. Dev lifted pushed the heavy tubs and set them aside so that Rabbi Beth could pass, and then stepped over them and in front of her to shove open the heavy door. He stepped out onto roof and then turned back and offered his hand to help Rabbi Beth step through the doorway, like out of a darkened theatre into the disorienting light of day.

Dev Brennan propped the heavy door with a wooden wedge cut for the purpose, and Rabbi Beth took a seat on the air conditioning unit near the reverse side of the leaded stained glass, a Star of David fifteen feet across that shone into the sanctuary in cobalt and claret. They could see all the way to the ocean. Rabbi Beth shielded her eyes with one arm and with her other arm pointed west, "There's Park La Brea," she told him. Tall now, unfolded, Dev Brennan lit his cigarette and inhaled. Beth shut her eyes and felt the warmth of the sun on her face. A breeze came up from the ocean and she realized for the first time that she wasn't nauseous. "That's Wilshire," Dev said. Beth opened her eyes as he talked through the exhale of his smoke. The smell of the cigarette was oddly appealing to her. Dev extended the smoke to her. She laughed. "Can't." she smiled. Then, "I'm pregnant." He studied her and a quiet smile appeared on his face. She felt herself suddenly proud and pleased. "I thought you might be," he said, bringing the cigarette back to his mouth, "you have that shiny hair." He held back, then patiently released the smoke from behind his lips. Each drifted, one forward and one back, to a place of contentment and they continued together in silent prayer. After a while, when Dev had crushed out his cigarette on the tar surface of the roof, he sat beside her and together they looked out over the sparkling city.

The Unveiling

"MY DEAR BELOVED," Iris began the letter to her husband, who would tomorrow be a year deceased. "Today in *shul* I sat between my parents. I lay the blame at your feet. The feet I would entangle with my smaller, colder ones, when you were considerate enough to be yet living. I sat between them, the widow, pitiful and angry for all to see. My parents, Jerome and Rose, sat taller in their seats, relieved to think that perhaps I would be noticed, and with that their hearts unburdened. Imagine their disappointment, that their daughter, not so pretty but pretty enough, pretty enough to have distracted you, made you flat out stupid on what became our first date, a trip to the 24 hour store in Cambridge for henna, no, cigarettes, the henna was an afterthought. But that's what we had told the children, the angels, don't get me started, so that they would not find it romantic to smoke. Imagine the disappointment of my parents that their daughter was theirs to carry once again and not just her, but also her children, who daily show their love in the form of anger. The boy, not yet ten, telling the grandfather to leave him the fuck alone and kicking him hard in the shins."

Iris Tellerman pulled her car into a space just feet from the five dollar valet, not because she was miserly like the rumor of the Jew, but because in the year since her husband died she could barely organize getting her kids to school in the morning, let alone a job. And though her husband had been smart about money and had had insurance from the union, Iris knew now, that you just don't know, and she had to be

53

careful. The house was paid for, but there was college and now it was all on her. "I am getting my hair colored today. I know you think it is beautiful and smoldering with a touch of grey, very Anne Bancroft, but it's not about you anymore. It's about taking my photos for JDate, because Melora says that I have to. 'It's been nearly a year,' she tells me, and tomorrow is the unveiling and I could meet someone, kidding. Or not—Melora might bring a guy from work."

Iris stepped into the salon where Melora had made the appointment and felt immediately steeped in a pleasant cynicism. She was none of the things that she needed to be to come here: not tall, not blonde, not vapid, not an actress. The man behind the desk had had his eyebrows waxed in a high arch that made him appear preternaturally interested. Iris gave him her name and continued her letter to her deceased husband. "The receptionist informed me while I waited, that for my first visit, I was being gifted with a twenty percent discount on a Brazilian wax. This is a gift. To have the most personal hedge of all shaped into topiary. Can you imagine it? Do you? The soft triangle that was easily covered by your hand, shaped to a valentine or a landing strip or removed completely to have the nectarine smooth surface of a porn star. Is this how I should make myself over for the lawyer who was cornered by my parents in a zone defense in the lobby of the sanctuary? Would he, in our breathless removal of each other's clothing, expect to slip his hand into the front of my jeans and find, nothing? Would the down you once petted offend? So be it. If that is what is called for, I will pour hot wax on myself and wrest it away at the root. Or better, not leave my house, nay my room, but to drive the children to school or to buy their food at Trader Joe's."

Iris stepped into the changing room and removed her t-shirt. Her breasts, she knew, were small but lovely, her body not so different than when she had gone to Camp Ramah as a teenager and been felt up by the very delicious Abram Scheinfeld, who she thought she heard was a rabbi now in Boulder. She unconsciously cupped her breasts beneath a bra she suspected it was time to replace and was posed that way when the perpetually surprised receptionist poked his head in and told her that Namaste was ready for her, the curtain drawn around his face like he was preparing to wash that man right out of his hair. "Namaste, for-merly Susan, suggested that I do a two-step process to add lowlights for warmth and to help brighten up my face, which she informed me was washed out by the unfortunate brown I was born with. This long-overdue transformation will cost, with blow-dry and tip, two hundred and sixty dollars, paid for by Melora who staged the intervention, be-cause 'I can't spend the rest of my life in the house with the kids.' That's what she thinks."

In the chair, Iris endured the smell of the peroxide and paged through the vacation album of Namaste and her dog Johnny Depp. He was one of the dogs now popular that were children-light and could be smuggled onto airplanes and into movie theatres like guns and popcorn, respectively. The album featured Namaste and Johnny Depp at various dog-friendly destinations: in the snow in matching down jackets, at the beach under a color wheel umbrella. They were well traveled and had plans for a visit to Nepal in the spring. Namaste and her assistant, Yzenia, guided Iris to the dryer as if she were both blind and clueless, each taking a hand. A third person, who was dressed in thigh-high striped stockings and platform Mary Janes like a saucer-eyed girl from a comic book, brought Iris a cup of Rooibos tea. For a moment, Iris thought she might leave her body and view the scene from above like her husband would if you ascribe to the floating above things version of death. She was relieved when they left her and, under the weight of the heavy *InStyle* magazines they had piled on her lap, Iris closed her eyes and resumed contact with her beloved.

"The children are well," she began. "We are like a small specialized unit—skilled at moving the groceries from the car to the house. Evan carries the heaviest things, like the man that he isn't, and Vered, with skill and precision, orders the couscous and macaroni boxes by height in the cabinet she makes tidy as a library. When she is done, Vered and I fold the bags and place them in a neat pile under the sink. I never have to tell them anything twice. They know it is just me, just us. We work together. I buy one special thing each for them when I shop. For Evan, it is Thai peanuts, and for Vered, fresh papaya with lime. After shopping, we snack on our treats and do homework. They both do their work at the dining room table and tuck the completed papers into their backpacks. They are uncomplaining and never whine. They do not dawdle or tarry like normal children. It is heartbreaking. Evan has a teacher this year who is a bastard. It is too much to tell you. He is punitive and mean and I would like to kill him with my hands. When I pleaded with him that Evan had recently lost his father, he countered that it had already been a year. I thanked him for pointing that out. I had lost track of it completely. I am teaching Evan how to deal with difficult people. The bad teacher is keeping Evan from the class trip to Space Camp because we have been late more than three times. Because there are some mornings when I open my eyes that it is too much and I have to shut them again and pull the blankets around me for a few more seconds to find my strength. Most mornings, all mornings, both children are in bed with me. It feels like we are riding a flimsy raft, but at least we are together." Namaste put her hand on Iris's shoulder and pushed the dryer back. Iris startled, it is that rare that someone touches her. "Do you want me to do those eyebrows?" Iris raised her hand protectively. No, she thought, I'll muddle through. "No thank you," she said. Yzenia guided her to the sink and rinsed the color from her hair.

"Do you remember before you were dead?" Iris continued, "Before you were sick even, when the children were small and we drove up to the redwoods? We were in the van and both kids were asleep in their car seats and the rain was coming down so hard that they kept closing the roads behind us. And we had that Van Morrison CD on that we would play when Evan was colicky? That's all. Just that day. I go back to it all the time. When we got back to LA, you got a pain in your shoulder you thought from playing basketball, and then it all happened like in a playbook. The diagnosis—the chemo. You know. You must have been sick already, but we didn't know. It was just our family then. It was all we ever wanted and the noise of the rain so loud outside and we couldn't see ten feet in front of us. And when we finally got there, after driving all that way, Evan and Vered refused to get out of the car to see the redwoods. They thought we were crazy and I guess we were. That is my perfect day. When I close my eyes on the mornings that are impossible, that is what I see. I can't believe you left me. I have to go. They are wrapping my head in a towel and wondering why I have tears running down my cheeks. Time for the big blow-dry."

Iris used the corner of the towel to dry her eyes and Namaste removed it like unwrapping a gift. Iris could see already that the color was beautiful and didn't know what to make of it. She looked like she had just come out of the lake at camp, her hair falling in long ringlets. Over the sound of the dryer Namaste stage whispered, "Is this a special occasion?" Iris resisted telling her the truth: that she was preparing to go to the cemetery and reveal the headstone of her year-dead husband. That after this she had to go to Neiman's and pick up the tasteful and appropriate dress that Melora had selected for the occasion, and panty hose and shoes that wouldn't sink into the damp earth at Forest Lawn. That she would pick up her sister-in-law and her husband and kids at the airport and that the housekeeper was due to vacuum the house and put the kids toys out of sight for the thirty or so people that would come back to her house tomorrow after the unveiling. She could see her mother already fluttering from kitchen to table, table to kitchen, interrupting her flight plan only to tuck Evan's shirt or adjust the hem of Vered's dress. If her husband were alive they would lie in bed afterward with the lights off and dish about Rose and Jerome, and his gentle laughter would make her like them better, relieved to be together in their quiet bedroom. He would bring her hand to his mouth and kiss it, and with the ease of a yawn pull her toward him, his arm hooked around her waist like a lifeguard. Iris let the warm air and the hum of the hairdryer lull her. She closed her eyes and remembered him in such detail that she caught her breath; her face flushed when she opened her eyes and saw herself in the mirror. Namaste stood back, pleased, and gave Iris a moment to take herself in. Her heart was still pounding from the dream of her husband, but it didn't alter or slow when she saw herself. A smile dawned on Namaste's face. "You see," drawing in her breath, "…beautiful." Iris brought her hand to the now cooling skin at her neck. In the mirror she saw the ring on her hand that belied that she was married to no one. Her hands moved to the sable smooth hair that cascaded down her shoulders. The room and the sounds around her receded and she felt a still quiet, like floating underwater her heart beating hard. "How dare you," she heard herself say under the rush of sound that broke over her. Iris reached down to the floor for her purse and quickly arranged a tip for Namaste, tucking the folded twenty into a tiny white envelope and dropping it into a box that Namaste had brought back from her trip to India where it was used for donations for orphans.

Iris walked back to her car and fumbled with the keys like she was being followed. When she finally managed the key in the lock, the alarm blared. From a high window of the Yeshiva near where she had parked, a group of students with *payis* gazed down at her from above like a human menorah. She pressed the button again, again, again until the alarm at last silenced and the minyan receded. Iris dropped into the driver's seat and locked the door behind her. She caught her breath as if she'd made a narrow escape and laid her head back on her seat, the air escaping her lungs in a stutter. She felt her hand clench in a fist and instructed herself to release it. Her husband was dead. She had known this before. She had, after all, attended his funeral. Had sat in the room at Cedars, had pressed her dry lips to his forehead, had released him. But for him to be dead still was too much. For a moment, Iris rocked herself to the sound of her own keening. Her head dropped against the wheel and two fat tears dropped onto her lap, and with that she righted herself. She sniffed and brought the back of her hand to the corner of her eyes. She knew well that her grief was useless. Her husband, day after day, remained dead. His children were proof of this. They were already taller, the shape of their very faces had changed. They ran and on days when they might be distracted, they laughed. He was not in this world. He had left her, left them, and Iris, as widow, was a reluctant expert. What she needed most to endure this loss was to rest briefly on the wide plane of her husband's chest. She was without him and her mastery had left her only weary only empty only angry.

Iris felt an impatient congregation urging her on. The celebrity of her husband's death now waning, novel only to her, when, before she opened her eyes each day, it jolted her limbs. They were eager for her to shed her grief like a viscose robe trailing off her fingertips. Iris was meant to step into a future she did not choose and did not plan for, a future that she could barely contrive, the exercise as useful to her as staring into the sun. "Who next will lift my hair and put his mouth on my neck? Who will trace the curve of my spine, place the flat of his palm on my belly? How close will you stand and allow this?" Iris demanded, "How will I race to him on stumbling legs?" Iris steadied herself, her hands holding the steering wheel of the parked car. "How I miss you," she said, "You who have left me to face my world to come." "What if I refuse? she asked, expecting no answer, "What if I don't unclutch the stone and lay it on your grave?" But Iris knew that tomorrow she would go and march as directed to mark the anniversary of her husband's passing. Then, with the sun catching the warm highlights in her hair, she would take the hands of her children, first one, and then the other, walk back across the soft lawn to the waiting cars, and after washing the dust of death from her hands, head back to the house for a nosh.

Iris gathered her hair in a ponytail holder that she found in the glove box and, pulling on Evan's baseball cap, she tucked her hair away. She started the car and put it in reverse. Then, pulling forward and easing her car out of the space, she drove north on Alta Vista, half-way down shearing off completely the rear-view mirror of a parked Prius. She pulled over, gathered the broken pieces from the street and placed them in the well of the passenger seat of her car. On the back of a lunch menu from Vered's school, she wrote in handwriting that was neat and easy to read, "Iris Tellerman," with her phone number and her promise to replace the broken mirror, which she knew from the last time would be about five hundred dollars.

New Jew

Nina Shepard had been a Jew for fifteen minutes. She sat at her table at the Ivy and regarded her soft-shell crab. She pushed it aside with her fork and then, setting her fork down, she reached for some bread. The bread was white and tasteless, laid unceremoniously in a basket with a napkin. Nina took a bite and set the rest on the small white plate to the left of her. She took a sip of iced tea and pretended to watch JLo at the table across from her on the patio as she waited for her mother to come back from the ladies' room.

Nina Shepard, a Jew, a Jewess, she wasn't sure, only that she was no longer Catholic, not really. That without having moved from her seat, or wandered through a desert, she became, without warning, a Jew. "Now that Poppy is gone, there is something I need to tell you," her mother had said. She had looked down at her butter lettuce salad, folded her sunglasses, and then, looking steadily across at Nina, her mother had given her this news. Her mother, who would bring Nina with her to choir rehearsals at church, where she played in the loft at eye-level with Jesus, speaking in a voice that still had music in it, told her daughter Nina, thirty-seven, with a daughter of her own, that now that her grandfather was dead it was safe to tell her. It was safe to tell her that Poppy, Sarah, and by extension (Judaism being matrilineal), she, Nina, were, had been, are now, and would be forever, Jews. Nina's mother returned from the ladies room, her lipstick freshened, and, snapping her purse closed, pressed her cheek to Nina's and said before leaving, "It doesn't have to change anything."

Nina had learned about the Nazis in high school and she remembered, even now, how relieved she had been to not be a Jew. She recalled the gratitude she felt at the pristine safety of who she was. Rachel Abramson had started to cry. She had gasped at the sight of the living skeletons reaching through the fence and then later at the mountain of shorn hair. When they showed the lampshade made of skin, Rachel had run from the room. Carol Held, not Nina, had gone out to the hall to comfort her. When the film ended, Nina had felt grateful that it had, and wondered only briefly how the Jews had let it happen. She had been moved mostly by the image of a small boy, on his sleeve sewn a golden star—*Juden*. And she wondered who had sewn it on, if he had been so marked by his mother's own hand.

When she was little, Nina would go to church with her grandfather. She had a beautiful lavender dress and white shoes. She would tuck her small hand in the crook of his arm and rest her face on his shoulder, almost as if she were cold, never looking past him to the brightly lit room, the sun in colors through the tall stained glass windows. His skin smelled of soap and like the clove-studded oranges of Christmas. He hid small blackberry pastilles in his palm and would silently reveal each one to her, resting in his hand like a pearl, so she would sit quietly in church, the candy a sweet secret between them. He liked to sit on the aisle in the corner near the door.

Karl Shepard had been a furrier, and in his store on Wilshire, Nina would lie on the octagonal ottoman and see herself reflected in the funhouse of mirrors that surrounded it. A delicious mélange of perfumes still floating on the cool air of the store long after the women who had admired themselves in coats of mink and sable had left the store. Nina, with her eyes closed, could recognize each pelt by touch: the arrows of the fox, the deep soft velvet of the beaver. She would come after school and listen as Poppy, with a voice that had a music of its own, soft and deferential, a whisper almost, as he took the arm of each woman who had arrived in a car with a driver from Beverly Hills and brought her to the fur that had been waiting for her all along. On his desk, he kept a box of cards with notes as detailed as a doctor's, with the birthdays of each of his clients and their preferences. Weeks before the occasion, he would invite a woman in, and they would walk the floor together to find the fur that would be hers. Like a perfect lover, he would hold the coat open and invite the woman in, the satin lining cool against her skin, the weight of the fur a sure embrace. When she had gone—lifted, ebullient—Poppy would phone the woman's husband at work. The men would come by at the end of the day, after five on the way home from the studio. Poppy would offer them a glass of scotch and their check he would place into the drawer of his desk as if it were an afterthought. Rising to shake their hands and to nod in agreement that pleasing one's wife was not mysterious, you only need give her what she wanted; Poppy, a trusted friend of both man and wife.

Recovering her car from the valet, Nina was momentarily disoriented by the flash of the paparazzi who camped out across the street. The car brought first was a Land Rover that belonged to a blonde who Nina didn't recognize, and a boyfriend with pants so smallish he looked like he had eaten the side of the mushroom that makes you suddenly taller. Her daughter, Annika, would know who they were and would admonish her later for not knowing. Nina, whose car had been pulled up, stood stock still—her daughter was Jewish. The valet had to resort to honking to get Nina's attention. She ignored the glares of the lunching women and tucked into her car, nearly forgetting to tip the valet with the five she clutched in her hand. She felt a new concern of how he would judge her if she had forgotten. She drove south on Robertson, suddenly without destination. Her daughter was at Immaculate Heart and she would not be ready for pickup until three. Distracted, Nina got going the wrong direction on San Vicente, and wondered how she could get lost in a place she had lived her whole life. She reversed herself at Wilshire, and drove east several blocks until finally she pulled over and sat in the parking lot of the 99 Cents store.

She left the engine running and tried to recover herself. "Now what?" She thought to call her husband, and taking her phone in hand stared at it like an archeological relic, as if its purpose was unknown to her. She set the mysterious object down on the passenger seat. She would wait until her husband came home that evening. She would tell him in their bedroom while he removed his tie and shook off his loafers. Even this seemed impossible. She remembered that her friend Eliza, who was in AA, had said that in moments when you are lost you are to "do the next indicated thing." But what was that? Nina had no idea. She started the already running car, apologizing to the passersby for the resulting scraping wail, and wanting to feel that she had some say, turned left and pointed her car north on Fairfax.

Nina had been to Fairfax before, had driven through. Once after a school play of Annika's the cast had gone late to Canter's, which they treated like Sardi's West. She pulled into the parking lot of the Diamond Bakery, and climbing out of the car was given a ticket by the valet, who was an Indian Sikh. His presence made her somehow feel less a stranger. Nina felt better walking, the rhythm of her feet on the ground reassuring. She stood in front of the bakery and reached to open the door. "You have such beautiful legs." A hand lay on her outstretched arm. Nina gasped. The owner of the hand, an eightysomething woman with a voice as low as a man's, grasped Nina's flesh more firmly. "I have my father's legs," she continued, nodding, as if this was something Nina should already know. The woman stood regarding her, waiting, Nina realized, for her to open the door. Nina stood back, and letting the woman go ahead of her, entered the bakery. Inside, it was impossible not to be reassured by the smell. Nina leaned back as the woman pulled a number from the red dispenser and felt that she had time traveled. The woman, seeing that Nina was not moving, pulled a second number from the machine and handed it to her. It was 18, and something about that seemed significant to Nina. Then, she remembered then that that was how Jews made gifts of money—in increments of eighteen…thirty-six, seventy-two. She had written a check for that amount for the Bat Mitzvah of a girl in Annika's class. The bakery was filled with women who all seemed to know each other. The one who had spoken to Nina, instructed the woman behind the counter to slice the rye thin, indicating the same with her fingers. A woman whose hair was so white it was nearly transparent entered the store in mini-steps, a young Ethiopian aide at her elbow. The woman behind the counter tied a pink box with string that she drew from a spool. Nina caught her own reflection in the mirror, her brown eyes and dark hair. The woman could have been her mother.

Nina's grandfather was fair. Light hair and green eyes. Nina realized at once that that is how he could have done it. How he could have gone to bed one night a Jew and woken the next morning a Christian. Nina realized how little she had known about her grandfather's life before he'd come to Los Angeles. Only that he had been an orphan. The details had not interested her. There would sometimes be fleeting references to the war, but Nina was like most children, uncurious about a life before her own, content to be with him, the object of his attention. From his house in Hancock Park, Poppy served another clientele. In the front room, magicians would come and sit. Poppy would open trunks and, from the same fur that draped the shoulders of the women at the store, he would form cunning white rabbits fitted with springs inside. Poppy would reveal the white rabbits crafted by his own hand and make them come alive. Nina would gasp with delight when the creature would stir, though she had seen Poppy sew the puppet with her own eyes, his hand drawing the neat stitches at the store. Nina, only ever pleased and willing to be deceived by him. The visiting men would sit in the parlor of Poppy's house and examine his wares with a keen eye, regarding them as unparalled treasures. The men who were always eager to please Nina by guessing a card she had chosen from an invisible deck, or plucking a rose for her from out of the air.

When Nina's number was called, she chose, without rhyme, a small box of cookies, and at the suggestion of the Ethiopian aide, a challah. The woman behind the counter handed it to Nina, her hand supporting it underneath like an infant, and Nina held the bag close, the fragrance rising. She felt like a child on a scavenger hunt. Stepping back out onto the street, Nina felt suddenly a rising sadness. She held the bread yet closer. Across the street, she saw through window of the Hirsh Family Kitchen, seated at the table, a group of men talking and laughing, their gestures broad and animated. The one nearest the window, smiled, listening, his head down and used a slice of challah to mop the soup in his bowl.

NINA RETURNED to her car and drove toward the temple on Hollywood Boulevard where she had once picked up Annika after the Bat Mitzvah of the girl in her class. Annika would not be the only Jew at Immaculate Heart. Of the student population that attended daily prayer, the Jewish students made up nearly a third. Nina slowed her car into a space across the street from the temple. The building was old, and she remembered driving by in the fall when the congregation spilled out after services flanked by security guards in suits, wearing earpieces, their eyes holding an attentive view of the periphery. She had been afraid for them—so many Jews in plain sight, vulnerable to any attack. She had stopped at the light and caught herself looking at them, wondering not if, but when, harm would come. Rising from her car, Nina regarded the building. It was different than other buildings in Los Angeles because it had weight, most of LA looking as if it were built that morning. This building was large and substantial, even the trees that surrounded it seemed more deeply rooted, as if the entire structure had been transported, flora intact, from Cleveland or New York, like a Jewish snowglobe.

The doors were open, and a guard, like the one she had seen before, stood at the door as people filed in. Nina racked her brain to remember if it were a Jewish holiday of some kind, knowing as she did that Hanukah rhymed with Christmas, Passover with Easter, but she could not recall any. Still, a small assembly of people were filing in. She realized, as she watched them, that the guard had begun to scrutinize her. That he not think ill of her and her purpose, Nina crossed the street and entered with the others. When she stepped past him, he smiled and gave his head a quick nod. He did not stop or question her. When the group she had followed reached the sanctuary, she hung back, remaining in the lobby illuminated in the half-light of the white Christmas bulbs repurposed as memorial lights. Nina started down a hall. Over an intercom she heard laughter, but she was otherwise alone. On the walls of the hallway were framed pictures recalling the temple's history. One held a photo of Elizabeth Taylor and Eddie Fisher. Another, a roofless temple filled with congregants attending High Holiday services while the then-new building was being constructed; the women wore hats with veils, coats with fur collars, coats of fur. Nina searched the photo, wondering which of the women had come to her grandfather's shop.

"I can't stand it either." Nina turned to see that a man her age, dressed in a suit, was standing beside her. She started at his sudden appearance; she had not heard his approach. She made no reply, but the man took her silence as agreement. "Some primitive ritual. I mean, tell me, if someone came after your infant with a blade," with this he made as if to prick the flesh of her arm, "would you allow it?" He answered his own question, " No, of course not." This time he tapped her arm to mark their shared belief. The man leaned over and took a sip of water from the small fountain set into the wall. Refreshed, he went on. "I'm the Sandek," he said to Nina, extending his hand to her and holding hers tight and firm, as if he has just sold her something. "I'll hold my nephew on my own lap, while they do this thing to him." He glad-handed her on the shoulder and then, tugging on the hem of his jacket, moved toward the door of the sanctuary. " What do you want to bet, when he grows up, he comes after me?" He smiled thinking of it and laughed to himself. He put his hand on the door and turning back to Nina said, " Nice talking with you," as if they had spoken. She stood a moment longer, when the sound of the rabbi's voice came over the intercom. She felt suddenly as though she were late for something and, following, stepped toward the door that the man in the suit had just stepped through.

The room Nina entered was expansive, at least three stories to the ceiling. At the front, a small gathering of perhaps twenty people stood together in a loose circle, the voice of the Rabbi conversational, the group attentive. She guided the door closed behind herself and slipped into a seat at the back where she was shadowed by an overhanging balcony. She unconsciously reached for a prayer book but remembered that this was not church and the words would mean nothing to her. She saw now that at the center of the gathering was the infant, held by a young father and the child's mother, who had the specific beauty of a woman who has recently given birth, awash in her own power and gratitude, a prayer herself. The infant was handed over to the Sandek she had met in the hall, who planted his feet, and took the baby with an expression that betrayed only pride and satisfaction. Nina remembered herself in the days after Annika was born. They had not even chosen a name, Nina lying on her side passing hours gazing at her daughter. Poppy was already old and living at Park La Brea, and they had brought the infant to him. He had held the baby and his breath. He had closed his eyes and weighed her. It was he who suggested the name, after whom, she wondered now. Because of course he had had parents. Nina felt a weight on her chest. How had she not wondered at it: a mother, of course a father, and a home... a younger sister. A younger sister. Nina drew in her breath, mourning a child she had not known. A person does not arrive in the world a man. He was first a child, a son. Nina placed her hand on the back of the chair in front of her to steady herself, knowing at once that she has been complicit in her grandfather's deception, playing a game with him as a small girl where he would challenge her to hide. "Quick, quick," he would say clapping hands after her, " They're coming." rewarding her with his pride and pleasure at her cleverness at tucking into the wicker hamper, the narrow closet, silent behind his heavy cashmere coats. Once, tucking into the linen closet, in the quiet of the cool dark sheets, Nina had fallen asleep. It had taken Poppy only a few more moments to find her but when he had, he had gathered her up suddenly and drew her to his chest where she had felt his strong heart pounding. He had kissed her on her sleeping eyes and she had felt his face wet with tears. "Sleep *tateh*," he had said to her, *"Mine tateh-Gey Shlofin."* Nina directed herself to imagine the truth she had not allowed her beloved grandfather, at once seeing a mother pacing in small steps in her kitchen near the stove. The woman is waiting for her husband to return from the police station. She worries the corner of her apron, drawing it to her hand in twists and knots. Finally, she is resolved. Nina sees now with breathtaking clarity as she examines her son and assessed that his wheat colored hair and green eyes flecked with gold would save him. She takes a coat that is warm, what food he can carry and pushes him with her own hand to start away. She stands at the edge of a dark forest, his infant sister in her arms, and lies to him with steady dark eyes that she and his father will come soon. But he knows and she knows that she will never come. A light gasp was drawn from the family and friends who stood around the new Jew and Nina, startled, caught her own breath. Nina rose from her seat and watched as the *moyel* offered a drop of wine to the infant. The mother had outstretched her arm as she unconsciously reached toward the infant, as if to stay the instrument, but in the end, had let it fall to her side, knowing, as she must, that she could not stop what lay ahead of him.

Nina stood to go. Annika would need to be picked up soon. She took silent steps on the balls of her feet, but the Sandek had seen her. He took a half step back and beckoned her to join them. She began to gesture that she must go but it was useless. He extended his hand to her and she moved toward the circle, which bubbled with the sounds of approval and the hearty claps against fabric of congratulation. She reached the Sandek and he opened his arm to her and drew her in. Nina was suddenly amongst them. The mother was to her left, retelling the story of the *bris* to those closest to her as if they had not been there, and they responded too as if it were all brilliant and new. There was laughter and tumult and the clean smell of starch and flowers that accompanies a celebration. The Sandek turned away from her and she thought that she would go and then he turned back and placed in her arms the infant. A mother, Nina could not help but accept the infant as an expert, making a bridge of her hand to support his head and bringing him closer to her body. Nina regarded the child, the smallest foot possible escaping the bonds of his father's attempted swaddling. The Sandek faced her, his eyes bright, expectant and full of pride. And Nina wanted to explain that she was not part of this family and that she did not belong here, that this precious baby was not hers to hold and protect, but she couldn't, because none of that was true.

Shomer

MY FATHER IS A CANTOR, an old school baritone with a voice that is a place. He is also a television executive, starting out as an entertainment lawyer and becoming later a producer and finally an Executive Producer on shows you've heard of, but on Rosh Hashanah and Yom Kippur he is a cantor, and Jews who grew up Conservative and cannot bear the thin sound of a woman's voice come to the temple to hear him pray. Sarah Silverman's sister is a rabbi—it's that kind of town. I bring my books with me from Oakwood and sit in the back of the sanctuary while he rehearses with Rabbi Beth. I'm good at math. I could do it for a living. I do it the way that some people doodle on a pad. I make a bridge with my knees on the back of the chair in the sanctuary and finish my calculus and once in while my father's voice is so stunning that I realize I am looking up at him, my pencil's poised in the middle of a separable differential equation and my mouth's a little open like I'm catching a breath. If you saw my father in the hall at the studio you would think he absolutely belonged there, but when he sings he is someone else altogether. He is like the glow from a warm fire in a temple in a shtetl and the rest of the world is cold as hell and your feet are wet and you are lying on the skylight of the temple longing to be inside. His voice is a place you want to go to. Rabbi Beth is incredibly pretty. She looks like a Jewish Snow White. When I was a little kid and she had just started, she would tell us Jewish folktales that didn't make sense and were impossible to follow. At the end, you felt dizzy like you'd been spun around wearing a blindfold. "One Friday night in a village there was a banquet and a beggar came in asking for food," she would start, "the people ignored him because his clothes were tattered. Then a prince came and the axle to his carriage broke in front of the house of the poor beggar." In the middle of her story there would always be another story, like Russian nesting dolls: the angel buried gold under the bridge; the tailor had a dream with the butcher in it; the son became a bear. I couldn't take my eyes off her. Somewhere in the middle of the story she would leap to a moral: "and that's why we don't gossip," or "that's why we give *tzedakah*." And she would look at us searchingly, hoping that we'd bought it. She would bite her lip a little. My mother had been dead only a few months when Rabbi Beth came to the temple and I thought for a while that I could get her to marry my father. But then she showed up with a husband who wasn't anything special as far as I could see, he couldn't even sing, and I mourned my mother in earnest.

The reason I would like to go to Princeton is that my mother, whose hair was the color of turning leaves, had wanted me to go there. Every year we would take a trip together to her parents' house in New Jersey and we would see autumn. Just my mother, my brother Jonah, and I. My father, who made all things possible, was never able to get away with us. My mother, Nava, would draw a rake across the lawn and look up at the wide sky and the trees as if she were listening. Together, we would stuff the leaves into black bags named for the purpose. The lawn was studded with piles of leaves; we would run and leap into them. She would laugh, but she would guard us, because a childhood friend of hers had been run over in that terrible way, hiding in a pile of leaves. When my brother died, my mother and I stayed in New Jersey for three weeks and in sweaters, with a cool in the air, we sat an extended *Shiva* at my grandparents' house. My grandmother was relentless and woke my mother early each day, forcing her to get dressed, sometimes drawing her up and out of bed with her own hands. Every day, friends of Zayde Jack and Tate Ruth who had known my mother when she was a girl would come and sit with her, sipping cups of Red Rose tea, quietly dipping mandel bread. They would, by way of comfort, tell stories of other losses, punctuated with *t-t-t* and *chas ve challelah* G-d forbid. I was nine, Jonah had been thirteen. My mother was thirty-seven.

WHEN PEOPLE LEARN that we have lost both my mother and my brother they react with a kind of consternation, as if tragedy and loss are meted out in a logical way. Steve Colbert lost his father and brother in a single day. In confirmation class, Rabbi Beth told us about a man who had lost his sister in the Twin Towers and when his father had learned the news he'd had a heart attack and died on the spot. This is what the world is, people reacting to what they have lost, wandering around, looking. If you sit in temple on Yom Kippur and say "who shall live and who shall die," you can be sure that someone to the right of you and to the left of you will die. Tragedy is newly invented every day. Look around the sanctuary—a woman with a baby in her arms lost her husband before the child was born. The baby has a shock of black hair and the mother studies the baby's face for her husband. She looks as if the baby was only just placed in her arms. She is still so lost. Shiva is just the beginning. The first year is just the beginning. My father went back to work right away, after Jonah and after my mother too. He dressed each day in a pressed blue shirt and sat with a cup of coffee and the *Los Angeles Times*. When it was just us, he would make my breakfast and would touch my shoulder to wake me. Our mornings were quiet, silent but for the turning pages of his paper. Before I would walk out the door for my ride, he would tip my chin and look at me. He would draw me to him and kiss my head. Then he would release me and send me out the door to school. I worked hard and did well, as you know, in spite of, not because of, teachers who regarded me shaking their heads, sometimes tears welling in their eyes.

WOMEN ADORED US. We could have never cooked a meal. They arrived every evening, bearing baskets with napkins wrapped around plastic forks, Tupperware containers filled with meatloaf and potatoes—a separate one for each. Always cookies. The women would duck in with a kind of curtsy, placing the basket on the island in the kitchen. They were often beautiful, their cheeks flushed as if they had come from a run. I had cello on Thursday nights and that is when he probably slept with them I realize only now, although he was discreet to the point of worry. Zayde Jack and Tate Ruth were the ones who introduced him to Marisa, at the wedding of cousin Ziggy's son Brett. Marisa was pretty and had eyes like blue water. She would look at me for a long while first and then, sometimes, push the hair out of my eyes. She played flute for the Los Angeles Philharmonic and invited us to see her summer evenings at the Hollywood Bowl. She would appear on the giant screen in a white blouse, a look of intention on her face. Although I was in love with her, my father was not. She left us and later married an engineer who worked at JPL.

After a while it became hard to imagine a person intruding on our home. Our evenings were quiet too. I did my math at the dining room table. My father would read scripts seated on the sofa, the remote in his hand, watching CNN. We had what my mother would have called a "companionable silence." And, in the space of it, my mother and Jonah still dwelled. Between us they were present and, although we left our house and went to dinners and parties and basketball games, we were both of us eager to return to this place because they had been here. Often, we would look up from our work and find each other. Our timing would affirm that we and only we knew what was so beautiful before. We, in that space, would travel to it—the portrait of our family: my mother's auburn hair falling to the top of my head, Jonah's head tossed back in laughter, my head pressed to Jonah's shoulder, my father enveloping us all.

Every day the world is new. The day before Jonah died there was one world. The following day there was a world without Jonah. There are a hundred Jewish stories in which the world makes sense. In the stories the wicked are punished and the good are rewarded. I don't need to tell you that this is not true. There is a story about Elijah, the Elijah who stealthily sips wine on Passover, in which the life and untimely death of a child changes the world. It is false to give meaning to death. The stories are to keep us from running into the streets and rending our clothes.

When my father prays he is both entirely present and completely remote. He is an agent for the entire congregation and when he prostrates himself in a white suit for Yom Kippur is it for the benefit of others. But when he does, when he lays his hands in front of the ark and gives himself over in surrender, in a vow of his helplessness, I see that he is as a child before God. I have lain on the floor of my room the way that my father has before the *bima*, in silence—the clear moon in my window like in a storybook—and I have prayed. I have prayed that my mother and Jonah will be restored to me. I have prayed with a weakness that my father does not die. I have prayed that he does not die.

I am in love with Maya. There is an idea that seventeen is too young to love someone, but that could not be less true. She has long dark hair and dark eyes and she is smarter than I am. She is compassionate and kind. She is funny in a way that is unexpected. We met last year when Rabbi Beth led the confirmation class on a trip to Israel. The classes flew to NY and left on EL AL with groups from all over the country. I first saw her at the airport leaning on her backpack, reading. I can't tell you what the book was because I only saw her. There was something about her hair falling forward as she leaned over, reading her book that she held against her knees. She kept pushing her hair back behind her ear and it was hard not to watch her. On the plane, she was laughing with her friends a few rows in front of me. For the rest of the trip I was able to find her by her laugh. We were in a place called Sde Boker— the desert where the Jews wandered—when I kissed her. We were lying on the ground looking at the stars and one by one the others left. I reached out and held her hand. I felt at home. She gave me the feeling of being in the right place, that the hard part was over. Her skin tastes like lemon and the saltiness of the beach. That is more than I should have told you, but I can't make myself delete it. I don't want to delete it. The air that night smelled of sage and the air in LA sometimes smells the same way. She will be going to NYU in the fall and if I am accepted to Princeton, I can get there by train.

WHAT I BELIEVE is that the presence of a person beside you has great power. It is why we pray together. Why we are proximate to each other. Why a minyan is called for. This is the work and the gift God gave to us. When we stand in the sanctuary and our sleeves brush the person beside us, that is God telling us we are not alone. After Jonah and after my mother died, ten people from the temple came to our house for seven days and made a sanctuary of our living room. Ten members of the congregation came and prayed in a room that looked out over the Hollywood Hills. When I would open my eyes after the *Sh'ma*, I might see a piece of the ocean sparkling on the edge of the shore, shimmering like mercury. The room was crowded with people *davening*. We stood shoulder to shoulder with ten people, some that we knew, and some, whose gift seemed yet greater, that we knew not at all.

When a Jewish person dies there is someone who is assigned to sit beside the body until it is buried the next day. The body is wrapped in white and treated with a mixture of egg white and vinegar. Shards of pottery are placed over the person's eyes. The *shomer*, who is a member of the burial society, sits near the body and recites Psalms. He is there to shepherd the soul, so that as it lingers it is not alone. He is there all night and his voice is a lullaby for the departing soul, the sound of comfort. So that we are not alone, God has given us each other.

I want to tell you about Jonah. I feel like I should tell you. It is hard to know me without him. It is impossible. Dad and Jonah and I had been hiking in the mountains of San Gregornio. It was summer and we were in shorts, but there was snow on the mountains and you could taste the snow on the air. I had been tired and wanted to rest. I was nine and Jonah was thirteen. All around you could hear the bees humming and it... it made you dreamy. We stopped by a beautiful clearing and there was a glassy lake. My father set the pack down and I ran to the lake's edge to put my feet in. We could not have hiked in too far, because we were children. It might have been under a mile. We had no cell phone, because my father meant the weekend to be like the kind he had spent with his own father. I walked back to my father, who was taking a sandwich out of the pack. We had the kind of canteen that has flannel and I twisted the top and took a drink. The water had a metallic taste that made the water seem colder. Jonah had been lying in the grass looking up at the sky and he cried out. You need to know that it was not the kind of cry that had alarm in it. "Damn it," he said. My father had not even looked up. "Jonah," he had said. He had admonished him for his language in the lightest way. A minute later, Jonah walked over to my dad and me. He moseyed. He was scratching at the sting with his fingernail. And then suddenly his eyes raced around frantically and his hand went to his throat. You know that he dies in this story. We all know that. My father dropped the pack and ran to Jonah. He made a decision in that split second that he would move faster without carrying his son, without me trailing behind. He told me to stay and he ran for help. Jonah, and I were alone in the middle of a grassy field and I stayed next to him and I talked to him. I was crying and was prattling on. I tried to be funny like my mother would be. "Way to spoil the camping trip, Jonah," I said, things like that, but I was scared, a baby really. I ran out of words. But then I looked at Jonah and his fear subsided altogether. He was my older brother. His eyes were at once calm and locked to mine. He knew that my father would not return in time. I will not describe the sound of his breathing or the color of his skin, because this is not a movie. It is the story of my only brother, who was dying. He held my hand and reassured me. When he died, I was alone in the meadow but I spoke to him. I lay down at his side and told the story of all our good days together and the *neshama* in him that lingered was for me, so that I would not be unguarded.

When my mother and I returned from her parents' house in New Jersey, she rented a house near the beach in Venice. She sat in a fabric chair with a metal frame and smoked Marlboro Lights. During the week I stayed with my father, because he was closest to school but on the weekend I would stay with her. No one spoke of divorce or something ending, we just carried on in this new way. I learned to make coffee. I would bring my mother a mug with half and half, and I would make a cup of tender coffee—milk and sugar with some coffee—for myself. She cried when she needed to, but it did not interrupt the flow of her words. We were friends in that time. She would hold her cigarette away from us and she would study me, push my hair aside with her free hand and warn me that I was becoming handsome. I would chop peppers and onions and together we would make dinners without my father. Afterward we would sit in our chairs wrapped in blankets and watch boats rock on the canals.

MY MOTHER RETURNED home and to my father a few months later. She traveled the halls of our house with caution. Taking half steps. But soon we were a version of a family who had dinner together on Shabbat, who sat pressed on the sofa to watch TV. My mother drove me to school and to practice. They discovered the cancer during a routine exam she had postponed because of Jonah's death. She died in weeks. After the second funeral, we came home to a house so empty it could not have been ours. The sounds of our own voices harsh and abrupt, we listened instead to our own heartbeats the taking and releasing of breath. We lived in this silence, so that a whisper was made by the knotting of my father's tie or the crisp falling of pages of my book, and then, when the prohibition of the first years mourning against singing was lifted, almost to the day, Rabbi Beth came to my father and asked him to sing.

He had said no, but she had pressed him. He was busy with work, he protested, but she insisted it was temporary, the beloved female cantor of thirty years was leaving and a search committee had been formed. In the end, he relented, right away consumed with it, setting scripts aside to review music. My mother's side of the bed was stacked with prayer books and books about prayer. He sat where he had read the paper and studied *trope* instead, humming the notes, his eyes guided by a silver *yad*, the one given by Zayde Jack to Jonah on his Bar Mitzvah.

We went together to the temple sanctuary, which was empty during the day. Fred, a pharmacist from Russia, who now ran the sound at the temple and arranged the microphones that were set up for the High Holidays, set the branch of the mic to the height of my father. I was in the back of the room and snaked around the empty aisles bored, distracted. Rabbi Beth, dressed in her street clothes, turned pages and spoke to Fred over the mic, like testing it for a play. She stepped down off the *bima* and walked into the sanctuary to where I played and my father stepped forward to the mic. I knew why we had come, but in those moments I had forgotten. And then my father sang. My father, whose voice might quaver with sorrow while saying good morning, sang. I stopped still. Rabbi Beth stepped beside me and lightly placed her hands on my shoulders. The wide sound of his voice opened and yearned into the corners of sanctuary. He sang and my bones vibrated. I let the sound roll over me and fill me and break the clay of silence that had held our lives.

Chavurah

SUSAN GREENBERG set the disposable Tupperware containers on the island in her kitchen. She opened the *Dorothy of Oz*-like picnic basket that had not been used since she went with Aaron and the kids to see the UCLA marching band play the 1812 at the Bowl how many summers ago. She set a dishtowel on the bottom—one from Sur la Table that she had purchased specifically for this purpose—and, in order of size, heaviest to lightest, she set out the meal that she had made for the woman in her *chavurah* that had breast cancer. Her name was Elisa Shapiro, and Susan knew she had two children in the preschool, and that, weeks before, she had been a script supervisor on *Weeds* but that now she was *that woman with two small children who had cancer* and Susan had to fight back tears. She barely knew the woman but still felt, as if, the loss of her, remembered seeing the woman's daughter on the yard of the preschool, her little fingers struggling to master the latch of the small gate. A little girl too small to lose her mother, she would certainly not remember her, or would remember her very little. She might remember one thing, like Susan's sister-in-law who lost her own mother at four and could only, with effort, recall the feeling of terry cloth around her as her mother gently drew a comb through her just-washed hair. Susan deftly lifted the now-cooled chocolate chip cookies that she could have bought but instead had made— measuring the brown sugar and pressing it with her fingers, beating the eggs after each addition and spending most of a day making batches ten minutes at a time, removing each cookie with care from the cooling rack—because this little girl's mother was dying and it was the least she could do. They had found the cancer late and it was already in her lymph nodes, but Susan had seen on Elisa's Facebook that she was positive, that the chemo was at the nadir and it could only get better, and that she had uploaded a picture of herself wearing a fez. Susan set each cookie one on top of the other, nesting, and pressed the container closed, the fragrance rising in a puff as she did.

Susan had gotten the email from Alison Steiner, who led the mitzvah corps and organized a schedule to bring meals when they were needed. This year, Susan was pressed into service for *Bikur Cholim*—the mitzvah of visiting the sick—when the choir leader had a low T-cell count, when Ayelet Halpern lost her mother and, the one that Susan most enjoyed, when Talia Abramson had twins. Susan had made a rich soup the way that her mother taught her, with a chicken she had procured from Western Kosher on Fairfax, carrots, dill, and parsnips. She had sent it with the *lokshen* in a separate container. Susan had also made tiny little meatballs with the unlikely secret recipe of ketchup and ginger ale, which she had requested from the mother of a friend in her own Day School when she'd stayed with the family for Shabbat. The meat was neck and tenderloin ground together with breadcrumbs from the challah Susan bought at Diamond. They were nourishing and delicious she knew; her own mother had made them for her when her daughter Dava, and later her son Gabe, were born. They nourished her as surely as sucking marrow from a bone. All the love she'd ever known was spoken through food.

Susan folded the doors of the basket closed like a book at the end of a story. She hooked the basket under her arm and carried it out to her car, a new white Accord that Aaron had bought her now that Gabe was off at Wesleyan. The car would stay clean, the days of the smell of French fries from In-N-Out and the musk of teen boy suddenly surprisingly behind her. She lay the basket on the seat and was guided by her GPS to the home of Elisa Shapiro in Hancock Park.

ELISA SHAPIRO vomited into a wastebasket lined with a Ralphs' bag and thought she was going to die. The thought made her laugh, "Oh wait, I *am* going to die." And the laugh threw off a last bit of spittle into a dishtowel she kept at hand on her bed, a place she once recalled making love with her husband in a position not nearly as acrobatic as the one she was in now, leaning out and over the bed to throw up, braced with one hand on the bed and the other on the facing wall. She finished the bout of throwing up, which made her wonder if she were specifically being punished for getting cancer. She laid back on her bed, more her home now than the rest of the house, which, she recalled, had a downstairs, a kitchen, a living room, a staircase strewn with toys, a room for a boy and a girl, Gideon and Lily, my darling, my sweetness. Elisa shut her eyes and felt grateful for the prescient wisdom of purchasing a Tempur-Pedic at twice the price, because the embrace of it, if she moves not at all, can quell the nausea for minutes. The bed is strewn with books that she cannot focus on, and a laptop so she can watch the dailies and be diverted by the sexy-fit Mary-Louise Parker, whose pot-selling adventures make her happy. Elisa smoked pot for the nausea, prescribed kindly by her doctor at Cedars; her beautiful husband Dan went to pick it up on Ventura Blvd. in Studio City, where legal pot distribution centers are as easily found as sushi bars. Elisa's friend Marla had picked up the children in a minivan with four booster seats. Dan came and sat beside Elisa on the bed with her and they had passed between them the government-rolled joint that was meant to quell her nausea and increase her appetite, but instead made her shoulders ache and made her briefly want to fuck her husband. Instead, they'd kissed across the array of books that covered his side of the bed by day. She'd admonished him for his sadness, which made him look sexier but acted as an unkind reflection of what he saw when he looked at her. "Marry the cute one whose husband had that aneurism last fall," she would say, and he would find her unfunny. "You know, the one who can still wear white jeans."

The pot helped her, but she only did it rarely because it made it hard for her to be with the kids the way she wanted to, to smell them, to listen to them breathe. Gideon, so male in his reaction to her, standing at a distance needing to be invited to sit on her bed, sometimes choosing to sit instead on the red plywood Eames chair, his feet folded underneath him like an Indian. He would read with patience to her from *Harry Potter*, thoughtfully changing register for the voice of Dumbledore, turning cross and sitting up straighter for Snape. Elisa sometimes struggled to keep her eyes open but did not want to miss Gideon's earnestness, his bangs falling softly across the lightning bolt she had drawn on his forehead with an old eyeliner; she would drink him if she could, the boy who lived. Lily, so easy and opposite, crawling feline onto the bed beside her, drawing her mother's arm around her like a cloak and telling Elisa with bubbling wonder that she loved Atticus, but that he did not love her and that he was as handsome as God and that he had fruit roll-ups in his lunch. Elisa was sure, without pessimism, that she would not live to be their mother. She had known it before she knew she had cancer. They had had Friday night supper at the Sobrals', the parents of Atticus. Lily had unabashedly curled her fingers into his hand, which he only tolerated. Claudia had made a beautiful dinner of roasted chicken with crisp salty skin and a sweet kugel with apricots. The children had their own table and tiny versions of the Shabbat table setting made from wood: a little challah, a diminutive bottle of wine. The actual wine was poured for the kiddish, which was made by Gideon, who stood like a Jewish Statue of Liberty and recited, with his pre-Bar Mitzvah-boy's voice, the blessing. After dinner, the children watched *Finding Nemo* in the living room and the parents sat at the table and railed against the Republicans and thanked God for Jon Stewart. Elisa had looked at the candles reflected in the window and knew suddenly that she would die soon. And the thing that puzzled her, with her two young children sitting close by unaware, was that she felt unsurprised and unafraid. She was startled when her husband's hand closed over her own, paper covers rock, and felt that she had betrayed him in some way. Before the next Shabbat, the doctor had found the lump and had excised it, had infused her body with all the best poisons. As if there was an opposite to remembering, she looked ahead and understood her death as a truth. Despite what she felt—that her death was inscribed—she fought entirely to survive. She understood that what was left of her was the story of her children's lives, that these days, hours and minutes were their story. That the narrative was to be taken up by them, which is why she pined for them when her friends took them late into the evening for play dates, misunderstanding that all she wanted was to be in their company, even without moving, even with her eyes closed only listening as downstairs in the kitchen, Dan clanging the small pot that was for making macaroni. Elisa felt the peacefulness of imagining their future. Dan, she knew, was a hottie, boyish and with each year more handsome, smile lines around his eyes as if squinting into a brilliant sun. She knew that someone would love her children and that in no more than three years, under the arbor in the backyard, he would remarry, Gideon standing beside Zayde Jack in a suit, and Lily raining petals in a path on the green grass. Elisa only learned she was dreaming when the doorbell rang.

Susan pressed on the doorbell gingerly and waited. When after a moment there was no answer she thought to ring it again, but didn't. She took steps back away from the door and regarded the lovely home. A princess flower brought a light shade to the porch, some of the violet petals fallen on the ground like a sudden mosaic. She drew the basket back to her and, stepping across the dark green lawn, made her way back toward the driveway and around to the side of the house. Across the back steps lay a boy's bicycle and, in the backyard, there stood a small castle made of plastic the colors of Chiclets; Susan knew that she was at least at the right house. She stepped up to the kitchen window, hoping to alert a housekeeper to her arrival. She raised her hand to knock but, peering in, saw no one, until she spotted Elisa making an uncertain journey down the stairs, one hand a guide on the banister, the other tracing the wall. Susan considered that she might retreat and make her way back to the front door, but Elisa glanced up and saw her. Elisa's expression was at first puzzled. Susan lifted the basket and brought it to her view and Elisa, doing the math of it signaled for her to wait and, in measured steps like walking on a rocking plank, she made her way to the door tying her robe as she came.

Susan took a quick breath in through her nose and drew herself up, cheerful but not frivolous, present but not demanding. The rules of visiting the sick were clear and prescribed: you are to come not early in the morning or late in the evening, you are not to bear bad news, you are to ask to be brought in. Elisa released the chain across the door with effort and, pulling her robe across her chest, swung open the kitchen door. "May I come in?" Susan asked. This is to give the person a sense of control, a choice, but it was so formal that it puzzled Elisa. "Yes, yes, come in," she said, but regarded Susan with curiosity, as if she had arrived from another time. Elisa felt somewhat as if she were still dreaming. Susan gestured to the fridge and Elisa nodded to her, catching up to the moment they are in now. "I'm Susan Greenberg," Susan said, and she rocked open the refrigerator door and then, with a surprising sense of ownership, began to put it to order, making space for each of the matching containers. "From the *chavurah*." "I don't know where Leticia is..." Elisa said, and looked around the room as if she had recently misplaced her. "She's gone to Gelson's," supplied Susan, which puzzled Elisa even more. Susan drew a note from under a refrigerator magnet and, careful not to disturb the family portrait done in wax crayon by Lily, handed it to Elisa, who took it in one hand, using the other to secure her robe, like pinning a corsage. "There's chicken enchiladas and a salad," Susan narrated as she placed the containers one on top of the other, "I made quesadillas for the children." And, having referred to them, Susan found herself grateful to be facing away into the cool air of the refrigerator. "And cookies," she made herself say cheerfully, as she looked up to distribute the moisture in her eyes that would be tears.

"I made some meatballs for you," Susan began, and opened the facing freezer door. Then, wheeling suddenly around said, "Unless you're hungry now." Elisa had just started to lower herself into the kitchen chair and Susan caught her halfway. Elisa stayed in this place between sitting and standing to check herself for the answer and Susan froze too, waiting for it. When Elisa said yes and time advanced, Susan found that she was elated, like she had won a prize. She knew she must contain that feeling, but it filled her in a way she cannot remember having felt before. Elisa began to tell Susan where the plates were, but Susan was ahead of her and, with the intuition of a woman who has made a home, she located without tries the lunch plates, the fork and napkin, the glasses. Susan prepared a small portion for each on two small plates. She didn't make conversation but allowed Elisa to rest in silence. They listened, both of them, to the ambient sounds of a bird in the yard and the hum of a mower next door. Susan knew that to sit at a table and share food is a great blessing and she set the table before them and in silence thanked God for his grace. Elisa regarded the five tiny meatballs on her plate and, with her fork, teased after one of them. A sweet smell rose in the steam and she felt an unfamiliar hunger. "They smell good," she said with a kind of surprise, and brought the food to her mouth. It was warm and nourishing, sweet and vinegary with something else, ginger. She looked up to find Susan watching her—they both laughed. "There's more in the freezer," said Susan, checking her pride, reminding herself that she is an agent of God and ersatz angel and that she is to be swift and undetectable.

"What is that…ginger?" Elisa asked, poising her fork for a second bite. "Ginger ale," Susan confided. "You're kidding." Elisa finished her second bite, hummed and tapped at the corners of her mouth with the napkin and then, having had her fill, sat back against the chair and closed her eyes. "I'm tired," she said. Susan stood and collected the dishes she had laid out. They heard the sound of a trunk closing. "I'll get these," said Susan, "go on up." And Elisa did, in measured steps like a climber, bringing her feet together on each landing and resting there before stepping to the next. Susan made quick work of rinsing and replacing the dishes. At the top of the stairs Elisa said "thanks," in a voice almost too quiet to hear and then, without turning back, raised her fingers in a wave. Susan, unable to find the reply that felt correct, in the end said nothing, but holding a damp dishtowel watched after her as Elisa disappeared up the stairs.

Susan recovered the empty basket and, pulling the door closed behind her, left the way that she came, walking almost on tiptoe down the drive. She was seen only by Lily, who had been skipping toward the door, but then stopped and regarded Susan with both curiosity and suspicion. In the end, Lily reasoned—when she had reached the safety of her threshold—that Susan was a good person and, before slipping into the house, granted Susan a small wave that was a scaled version of her mother's.

UPSTAIRS, Elisa pulled the summer-weight down quilt around her, adjusted the terry cloth cloche that was her at-home attire, and listened with great pleasure to the routine of the children's return and, at ease that they were under her roof, allowed herself to sleep.

SUSAN DROVE NORTH on Highland and had advanced more than a few lights before she attended to her surroundings, reliving the distinct satisfaction she had felt when the food she had made was eaten; the moment of undistracted pleasure she had seen on the face of the young mother as she had tasted the warm, delicious food. She thought of and then tried not to think of Dava. She had developed a discipline of limiting such thoughts because of the keen pain they brought her. She knew that Dava was a state away in Colorado. Unwittingly, she pictured the front door of the house she had found on Google Earth. Unbelievably, almost as if she had made it happen with the will of her yearning, the child, who she knew was her grandchild, had been captured running in front of the house—her hair lifted, her hands in vigorous fists, pumping forever the too-thin air. Captured in motion, the image had the quality of a watercolor, the girl's yellow shirt blurred like a streaking bird, her features softened, but recognized by Susan, so like the child she had raised. When she had found the image, Susan had cried out. It was a miracle she had kept secret, afraid that to utter it would cause it to vanish. She could open the page whenever she wished, but limited herself to once a day so that its stunning effect would not diminish. She knew that the child had grown, but she was in the picture, frozen in time. Susan, on more than one occasion, had reached her hand to the screen as if through it. Susan had thought that finding the picture was a sign, a God's eye view of the child she wished to console that she would someday be forgiven. Susan had left Dava's father, but it was Dava who had left Susan—frozen, like the screen image of her daughter, Dava was forever a teenager fueled with anger. Susan thought again of little Lily, her fingers curled, her step into the doorway paused as she turned, her eyes lit with friendship and recognition as she waved. Susan let herself hope that the child's mother would be healed.

To quiet her own aching, Susan thought of dill, the grassy leaves that floated in her mother's soup, and wished to have some—to roll it between her fingertips and be transported. She wished to take hold of a bunch of carrots and twist the tops so that the earth and sweetness were released in them. She wished to touch the brown paper of the onion skin and to cry while she cleaved it. She traveled west on Rosewood and made her way to Fairfax, where she found a space waiting for her. At Western Kosher Susan carried the chicken in her arms and balanced the parsnips and carrots and dill against her own body, impatient to begin cooking, to heat the pot to roiling, to skim the surface and fill her still house with comfort.

STANDING IN Western Kosher, Elisa adjusted the elastic under her wig and tugged at the false bangs that made her look like *"That Girl."* It suddenly occurred to her that the butcher had taken her wig to be a sheitel and believes her to be *daahti*—Orthodox, like the other women in the store, who each have six or seven children trailing behind them like ducks. Beneath her wig are the chemo curls that she never had before, the ringlets pressed against her head like the pressed, wet curls of a newly-born infant. Elisa said *"Todah,"* which is all the Hebrew she knew, and took possession of the ground meat that she will need to make the little meatballs, which, it turns out, is all she wants to eat, the ginger and sweetness of the ketchup somehow cutting through the nausea and giving her appetite. Alison Steiner had e-mailed and asked who had prepared and brought them in the rotation of meals during the chemo. It had turned out not to be Monica Albrecht from the Sisterhood, as she had first thought, or the gay dads from the preschool who had brought Chicken Cordon Bleu, but Susan Greenberg, the woman from the *chavurah*, Elisa misremembering so much from that time. Elisa paid, handing her Amex to a cashier, who was careful not to touch her during the transaction. She stepped out onto the sidewalk with her bags in a funny rolling cart. It was still difficult to carry, but less so to pull. She felt happily anonymous in her wig. She walked the few steps across the block to the Diamond Bakery and, seeing herself reflected in the store's glass, smiled to find herself there. She had not died after all, and remembered how inviting it had seemed to believe her own premonition. She wondered how she had been so fooled. She had been laying in her bed, the house darkening as the day receded and at a distance she heard Dan and the children laughing, their voices like light bells traveling up the kitchen stair. Elisa was pressed into her bed with weariness, but her attention went to the kitchen table, and she yearned to be with them in a way that was its own new pain. And she became suddenly angry, ferocious. A heat made its way from her core and into her limbs. She knew that she had been deceived, had been lied to. She knew at once that her that her future was no more written than her next breath. And pressing herself up with her the strength of her own arms, she inhaled deeply, and, with an intention that she learned from childbirth, decided she might live.

In the bakery, holding her paper number in her hand, she rested on the padded bench and listened to the voices of Jews sharing the news of this one and that one. Letting the smell of everything sweet surround her, she waited her turn. She would buy cookies for the children and challah for her recipe only from this bakery, and she couldn't use it today, only a day later. She would grate an onion and press the bread and meat together and, looking over her shoulder so that no one would learn the secret, pour in a cup of ketchup and a can of ginger ale.

Children are a Blessing

BERNIE ZISKIN SITS at his regular table at the Farmers Market in the cradle of Bob's Donuts and Patsy's Pizza. The voices of tourists and citizens of L.A. blend together in a walla that comforts him, reminding his body, but not his mind, of his childhood in Atlantic City, the summer air scented with baking raised glazed and pizza crust. His body has the ease of a boy sitting beside a friend. The market is crowded. A young mother sits beside him with her children, two boys and a girl. The boys, squirrely, are familiar to him. The younger boy is sitting on the wooden folding chair as if it were just a suggestion. A man Bernie does not know waves at him, his eyes oddly eager, mistaking him apparently for someone else. Bernie is hungry. In his hand is a three-by-five index card coated in plastic like a recipe; written in black letters is the name "Rosie." Bernie flips the white card, which reads "Will be right back." "Rosie," he tells himself, "will be right back."

The mother of the boys tries, with less energy than the task requires, to settle them down. The youngest upends the chair as he lurches across the table for a cruller. "Boys," she offers to Bernie by way of apology. Bernie smiles with genuine patience. "I have boys myself," then, "and a girl." A look of concern crosses his face. "A little girl." The mother, who is wiping the face of her little girl with a paper napkin that she licks to moisten, asks Bernie if he is from L.A. "I'm from Atlantic City. I've lived here thirty-five years." He feels hungry and the smell of the donuts and pizza is good. He is distracted by a flash of white and notices the white index card in his hand. "Rosie," it says. The paper has been made soft by his handling of it. He turns it over and sees, "Will be right back." He flips it back and forth, back and forth. "Rosie," he learns, "will be right back."

There is a family next to him with two boys and a girl. The younger boy stands abruptly and knocks over a cafeteria-sized carton of milk, which spreads across the blue table like a white lake. The mother tries to mop the spill with too-small paper napkins. Bernie catches her eye. She is exasperated. "I have boys myself..." and then with a feeling of unbearable sadness he remembers, "and a girl." His chest tightens and his eyes fill with tears. "Are you alright?" asks the mother. She holds the milk-soggy napkins away from her body and walks toward the trash bin, passing close to his table. "Yes," Bernie tells her. He is alright. His eyes are watering like they sometimes do. He shakes his shoulders because his chest feels a little tight, presses the heel of his hand to his sternum. "Are you visiting L.A.?" he asks cheerfully. He likes children. The boys are walking off to get ice cream and the little girl sits beside her mother, her small fingers drawing out French fries from a haystack on a paper plate. She licks the salt off her fingers. "I'm from Atlantic City. I've lived here for thirty-five years." The mother reaches out and describes a circle with the palm of her hand on the child's back. "What brought you out here?" asks the mother, and she looks at him but also at the children waiting for their cones at Bennett's. "I'm a lawyer. Entertainment law. I work over at the Paramount Studios right there on Melrose." He gestures east and then regards the table. If he is to get back to the studio on time, he'll need to eat soon.

The boys return with their ice creams and the older boy extends his fist sprouting dollar bills. Bernie feels a discomfort in his body and searches the market. He is waiting for someone and he is hungry. His gaze lands on the face of a woman working the counter at Moshe's and she smiles and waves at him with absurd enthusiasm. Why would she wave at him that way? He is uncomfortable, hungry. "Where is Rosie?" he asks himself. The name Rosie is in his mind like the solution to a puzzle. "Everything is Rosy," he hums to himself. He looks out at the people milling in the market. His hand clutches an index card. "Will be right back" is written on the card. Who will be right back? he wonders. He turns the card over again and sees a name written there—Rosie. And he feels suddenly that everything will be alright.

"Bernie, this is my husband, Jeff." He doesn't recall telling this woman his name, but he sometimes forgets little things. "Jeff, this is Bernie." The woman's husband has a plate of enchiladas. That is what Bernie wants. He is hungry. The father tells the boys to clear their plates and the boys respond to him dutifully, differently than to the mother. It was like that with his children. Ben and the other one. The one with green eyes. The one who liked to play outside. He searches for the name, which seems to elude him like a kite string lifting just out of reach. "I have boys myself," says Bernie, and then Bernie is suddenly overwhelmed with sadness. He remembers his daughter and he remembers that he had had to identify her body. Caroline. Bernie's eyes fill with tears; his chest tightens. He sees that the little girl has stopped eating and is looking up at him. "Why are you crying?" she asks him. He wonders why she would say this to him. "I'm not crying," he assures her, but he touches his cheek and it is wet. The mother offers him a paper napkin and he pats his own cheek. "Allergies," suggests the mother. The little girl tucks into her mother, making a shawl of her arm. "I have a little girl," he says brightly. "A little girl just like you. Her name is…" The little girl thinks a joke is being played. "You don't know her name?" Her mother presses down on her thigh in a way that startles the little girl. "I do," says Bernie.

He knows her name. The police who came to the door said her name. Caroline Ziskin. He sees them and feels the cool air of the night on his skin. "I have to get to the station." Bernie stands urgently. He pats his pockets for his keys but doesn't find them. Instead he finds another card with his own name written on it and his address. He regards the card and places it back in his pocket, but the child has seen it. "He's like Paddington. He's like the bear." "That's right," says the mother, her voice instructive like a teacher. She is craning to find in the crowd the person who must know Bernie. She attends now to his clothing and sees that it is clean. Someone cares for him, but they are not here now.

"I sometimes forget things," he says, almost whispering, and he is suddenly very tired. "We all do," says the mother in a tone that's light and reassuring. "Like Mommy's keys?" chimes the little girl. "Once we found them in the hamper."

Two boys come to the table and take their seats, the older one straddling the folding chair like a saddle. "I have boys myself, and a little girl." And he remembers her bare feet standing on his shined leather shoes. Her small hands in his, dancing this way in the kitchen. He recalls bending over to kiss her cheek and the rough of his beard against her new skin making her pull away laughing. "Caroline," the little girl supplies. "That's right. Her name is Caroline. She's about your age." The boys stand to go but the mother lingers. "You go on ahead," she says to her husband, who takes the little girl and the boys away, guiding them by the tops of their shoulders, looking back at the mother. "I want to stay and talk to Bernie."

"How do you know my name?" he asks, angry, suspicious. "You told me earlier," says the woman. "It must have slipped your mind. That's all." Bernie slows his breathing because the woman seems gentle and she reaches her hand out to touch the top of his and she does this with kindness. "Are you visiting L.A.?" he offers. "I'm from Atlantic City, I've lived here for thirty-five years." "We've just moved here from New York," the woman tells him. "I'm from Atlantic City. I moved here to work at Paramount. Right here on Melrose." He looks more closely at the woman because she seems familiar to him and she knows his name. "Do you have any children?" he asks her. "I do," she says. "I have two boys and a little girl." "I had a little girl once," he says, "but she died." "I'm so sorry," offers the mother. "We'll be sitting *shiva* at the house, please come," he says and takes her hand in his, his eyes brimming with tears.

Rosie returns to the table where Bernie and the mother are sitting. "I'm back," she says forcefully. She places a tray on the table in front of Bernie with a plate of enchiladas and fried plantains. The mother rises. "It was a long line, now that they opened the Grove," Rosie explains defensively. The woman leans forward and extends her hand to Bernie. "It was nice talking with you," she says. Bernie takes the object used for eating that is made of metal and places a bite of the warm food in his mouth. The man from the donut shop walks by with a white apron double-knotted around his waist and waves to Bernie. "Why would he wave to me?" Bernie wonders. "He doesn't even know me."

Keter Emmet

For nearly a month it had been crowns, inhabiting Becca's dreams and waking hours, images of crowns. When she was on hold with the airlines, booking her flight from LA to New York she had, she discovered, drawn perhaps a hundred of them. Before crowns it had been pomegranates, which she realized when she thought about it, had little crowns themselves, splayed from the top of each like a tree of kings. She had been right about the pomegranates and before long they were everywhere—on wallpaper, in hand cream, and tossed into salads. She had seen it coming. Now, when her eyes were shut and when they were open, she saw crowns. She wanted to tell her husband, so that he would be pleased with her prescience, like the time she had mailed herself a letter correctly predicting the sex of their baby, but she didn't. Somehow this information felt different, like it needed to be protected. Knowing that her husband might/would tease her that she was like what's-his-name in *Close Encounters*, Richard Dreyfuss, and soon she would be sculpting mashed potatoes and that she would have to defend herself saying, "Stop it. This is serious," and then where would she be.

Becca began to see one crown in particular that she knew she had to make. It was to be pounded by hand from soft gold, the edges unfinished, like a piecrust. She imagined the warmth of the gold, as she pounded it with a tool that she didn't know the name of which had been, thoughtfully, included within the vision, something like a one-handed rolling pin. She thought of ways to get out of it. Becca had not believed in God for at least ten years. She wondered how anyone could. Her husband was smug about it, having abandoned religion altogether as an adolescent, educated by nuns who he could intimidate with his sixth grade worldliness and height. Becca had allowed herself to misinterpret his lack of faith, believing that it would give her room to raise her children as Jews—a decision they came to in an underground parking garage in Century City after maybe their fifth date. Becca wasn't sure when God slipped away, but it was well before 9/11 and sometime after she noticed that good was only ever accidentally rewarded and that human beings were utterly without protection. She wasn't angry like Job; she knew by now there was no one to rail at. She thought it was something everyone must know and that persistently mentioning God in prayer was basically an agreement, like keeping up the pretense of a marriage for the sake of the children. And, although thinking about it sometimes made her nostalgic for the time when she did believe, she knew in her heart to a certainty that no one was coming, that the crimes of evil men—and by men she meant men—would go on unchecked, unless by some mistake they were interrupted.

This is why the visions were so troubling. The crown was by now inscribed in Hebrew letters that she knew from her eight years of Jewish Day School were *Keter Emet*, which meant, literally, crown and truth; knowing this made her feel suddenly sad and desperate, and she hoped like hell she had a mental illness. She felt, she admitted, as if God—in whom she did not believe—had chosen her and that she was a reluctant prophet and that this was consistent with the *Diagnostic and Statistical Manual of Mental Disorders'* definition of religious delusion that she had Googled. But as she otherwise failed to meet the criteria of a temporary psychotic disorder and post-partum was out of the question, she erased her recent searches and tried to let it go.

When the crown appeared to her she would place it on a cloud and let it float away the way she had learned in yoga. If it came back again, she would distract herself and have something to eat. She managed this way for perhaps a week when, at the Farmer's Market in the middle of eating a raised glazed donut from Bob's, she ran into her friend Sarah from the temple. Sarah told her about her new job downtown at a place

Becca had never heard of. And with the soft sweet bread in her mouth, Becca stopped still, her heart pounding, as Sarah clarified, "You know, the tall building downtown, the one with the crown on top."

And then, as swiftly as it came, the image disappeared. Becca's thoughts were once again blissfully occupied with needing to buy paper towels and dishwasher soap, a gift for her niece's twenty-first birthday, and remembering to TiVo *Weeds*. She drove on the 405 and the 134 and would go sometimes three or four exits thinking of nothing at all, noticing suddenly the startling pink of a bougainvillea on the side of the freeway and not even knowing for sure how she'd gotten all the way to her exit at Coldwater.

And that is why she was so unprepared when she sat in the sanctuary on *Kol Nidre* and heard the bells. It was evening and the ark was open and entirely empty. On the *bima*, instead of the rabbi and board members, sat a cellist from the Los Angeles Philharmonic who bore a heartbreaking resemblance to Daniel Pearl. He played the mournful and beautiful melody of the prayer; the lights of the sanctuary were lowered. The congregation of nearly a thousand rose and turned to the sound of the bells, light and simple like the sound of a shepherd mustering his flock, made by the carrying of the Torahs swaddled in velvet and satin, the smaller ones capped with finials—*rimonim*—the largest adorned by a crown. Becca kept her eyes trained on each of the Torahs as they were lain gently into the marble ark protected by carved lions as white as salt. Each lion rearing; between their paws, a crown pounded of soft gold— a crown that Becca had seen in her mind's eye and now before her. As the last of the scrolls was placed, she felt her heart catch and release like a mother laying down a sleeping infant. Relieved, she lowered herself into her chair and was comforted by the steady sound of her own breathing.

When she came back the following morning, hours before services, she was stopped by Security, a young man whose name Becca knew was Gustavo Esteban. The children called him Gus. Becca said hello to him and asked after his wife, Estella, whom she knew was pregnant. Estella, a nurse at Cedars, did cardiac ultrasound in the NICU. Gus had confided in Beth that, as the day grew near, Estella was more quiet and afraid for all she had seen—infants as small as a father's hand, with hearts like hummingbirds. Beth made a point each time she saw him of greeting Gus, because she knew that if some day someone meant to do harm, he would be the one in harm's way. He had told her that his mother had worked for a Jewish family as a maid and that on Fridays the father of the household would make up a box of food, *kugel*, and roast chicken for his mother to take home for Gustavo and his sisters. And while Becca knew that not all Jews were necessarily generous—he might as easily have been a *ganif*—she was grateful that this family had been. God or no, she was aware that when she left the house in the morning she was a Jew. As her hand grazed the doorpost, she knew that how she conducted herself in the world mattered. Because Gus knew her, he allowed her in, even without the key tag that had been mailed with her High Holiday tickets. He did not ask her why she was entering the temple so early in the morning, and she would not have been able to tell him, because although she had not slept and had made herself wait the two hours after the sun came up, she didn't know why she was there.

The temple was like a second home to her, familiar in its smell, a twin to the synagogue of her youth, where during Rosh Hashana and Yom Kippur she hung out with the other Jewish teenagers on the stairs, leaning back on the railing and laughing with the boys she would forget to marry.

Becca entered the Sanctuary from the back, where a box of black satin yarmulkes sat dutifully waiting in a straw basket, the inside of each emblazoned with gold letters: the Bat Mitzvah of Shelly Abramson; The Wedding of Rachel and Yoni; In Loving Memory of Rena Shapiro, Hillside Memorial Sanctuary. The same Hillside issued the Jewish calendar she kept in a drawer in the kitchen with old keys and pieces of chalk and only referred to when she was planning the trip back to New York at Easter/Passover. Becca leaned her body full onto the heavy wooden door and stepped into the empty sanctuary.

She had joined the Temple because of this room. She felt small in it. The three- story-high ceilings were cool marble; the green velvet chairs like an empty forest. The sanctuary was lit only by the daylight coming through the stained glass windows depicting the twelve tribes; some she knew, others she didn't. Asher, Dan, Levi, wheat, a scale, a ship with oars. The temple was built in the late forties and it had weight. When Becca and her husband had visited the Day School, the Principal told them, while standing in the sanctuary, without a touch of irony, that Nussbaum, the temple's first rabbi, had himself rescued the smallest Torah in the ark from a burning building during Kristelnacht, and also that he had converted Elizabeth Taylor so that she could marry Eddie Cantor. The principal pointed out that the eternal flame that hung over the ark had been a gift of Hal Wallis, the producer of *Casablanca*, that the stone image of hands held out in blessing had been the inspiration for temple member Leonard Nimoy when imagining the gesture for Spock.

In the empty room, Becca made her way to her assigned seat for the holiday and gazed ahead at the marble ark. Below the closed pewter doors, in gold letters in Hebrew were the words *"Dah Lefneh Me Ata Omed"*—"Know before whom you stand." When she thought of the warning she tried like a child to be good, to be worthy. But, she thought, her deeds were not measured by God. She knew that when she served food cheerfully to the old Jews at the Hirsh Kitchen and offered them a choice between chicken and chicken, that between them, in that moment of laughter, there might be some God. That when she cared for her children and tried to bravely love her husband, that might be God too. That what mattered was only how we treated each other and that that mattered because it was all there was. And that love and kindness was not a talisman from harm, it was only the brief beauty of love and kindness, so that when the harm came you would have known the other.

Becca had been on the *bima* only twice: her nephew's Bar Mitzvah, when she nearly fainted because of low blood sugar, and as a girl in pink tights, transported by the fragrant *besamim* of *Havdalah*. And, although she could not recall the journey from her seat to where she was now, she stood there with surprising ownership and trained her hands on the doors of the ark.

First letting her fingertips graze the burgundy velvet of the cover,

Becca took hold of the largest Torah. Bending at the knees, she lifted it to her shoulder. Laying against her body, the scroll had the terrifying weight of love, fragile and dependant. She knew that if she were to drop it she and the entire congregation would fast for sixty days. This had been the dare of her childhood when her brother was given the honor.

Becca closed her eyes as if listening and willed herself the strength to hold the heaviest of the four. She took short deliberate breaths, her hands white around the wooden dowels, the flat of her shoulder supporting the crown. And this is how she stood when Gus found her, a *tallis* held to his face against the smoke. He understood immediately that she meant to rescue the scrolls. Beth's eyes opened and stung; the air she drew in was harsh and worthless. She coughed and Gus pressed the *tallis* to her face. A grey cloud unfurled toward them down the aisles, roiling and angry like the sea consuming the Egyptians.

Gus took hold of two of the scrolls in one gesture, urging Becca forward, each regretting the fourth that remain nestled in the ark unaware. Rebbeca hefted the Torah higher on her shoulder and instructed her legs to step step step—as deliberate as math. She looked behind her at Gus, who held his breath against the smoke and directed her to the stairs behind the *bima*. Around her, Becca heard the popping and cracking of splitting wood and shattered glass. She disallowed herself a look back, but pushed her body forward. She could not see the stairs but took them running. Her thoughts, rapid and disordered, "thank God—who would do this—the children were not in school." She tasted salt in her mouth. Her face wet, she only then realized, from tears. Together Becca and Gus pressed open the doors to the preschool yard.

They were at once surrounded, the fire department having been alerted by the smoke alarm when the electrical fire started due to faulty wiring in the sound equipment set up for the High Holiday choir. A fireman Becca recognized from a school field trip took the scroll from her; relieved of its weight, Becca felt as if her arms might float on their own skyward. A young female paramedic wrapped Becca in a foil blanket and placed a plastic mask onto her face. Becca was made to stay seated in the open doors of the ambulance where the three Torahs lay on a gurney. She watched as Gus lifted his mask to describe to the captain where he would find the ark. Removing her mask, relieved by the sweet cold oxygen, Becca watched as a firefighter with the lumbering steps of a *golem* returned to the temple after the last of the scrolls. Gus stepped over the tangle of hoses to his car and returned to the ambulance a moment later with his Thermos and a brown paper bag of *pan de huevos*. He poured tea into the single handled cap and offered it to Becca, who accepted it, brought it to her mouth and sipped gingerly. Together they watched as the firefighter reappeared in the doorway, the final scroll in his arms. Becca dipped the sweet bread in the tea, the smell of anise floating on the steam.

Ariela Mireya Esteban was born that winter smooth and whole. On *Día de los Reyes*, Becca and her family had dinner with Gustavo, Estella and the new baby, in the kitchen of their apartment in Boyle Heights. In Becca's portion of the *Rosca de Reyes*—the bread of crowns—she found the hidden coin, which meant that the next meal was hers to prepare. When they came to Becca's house in Hancock Park, Gustavo brought Ariela in from the car in a carrier where she lay dreaming in her *Petit Bateau* onesie, a gift from the Sisterhood. And when she started fussing, Becca took the baby from Estella so that the new parents could eat their dinner. Becca raised the baby to the plane of her shoulder and felt just the warmth of her. She weighed like... nothing.

T'shuva

"THIS ISN'T MY FIRST REHAB." Adina looked down at her hands as if there were something there for her; they were cupped as if she were holding a bird. "It isn't even my fifth." She laughed and did not look up, only gazing again at her hands, raising them now as if bringing water to her mouth and lowering them again. "Did you know?" she said brightly, looking up suddenly, directly at Rabbi Dovid like an eager student. "Did you know, there was this guy once who jumped out of a plane with a backpack filled with cocaine. So anyway, the fall killed him and his backpack was left hanging from a tree. So this bear found it and ate the cocaine, all of it, he didn't stop 'till he had a heart attack and died. That's who I am. I'm the bear." "But you didn't die," offered Rabbi Dovid, "You lived." Adina tipped her head and brought her cupped hands to a chest like a vow, "Trying to," she said. She blushed like a girl, her skin already glowing pink from the rising sun. Rabbi Dovid rose and clapped his hands against his thighs, signaling that it was time to enter the Malibu surf. His group gathered there each Friday at lifeguard stand 17 where, twenty years before, he had sprinkled the ashes of his brother Eytan, whose request to be cremated was honored against the objections of their mother. Dovid had done it for him because he had asked him to, when he had called him from a bus station in the ironically named Needles. Eytan had been crying and said that he was done. The family had prayed that night that he would be arrested, but he had not been, and had died instead alone, some hours later, in the plywood living room of an unfinished house. That had been twenty years ago, when Jews were only good, before Jews had drug problems, before the doors of Beit T'shuva opened on Venice and Vera by the Jews of Los Angeles for their quietly broken children.

Adina guided the longboard into the dark cool water. She felt protected in her wetsuit, official, a person with purpose. Anyone riding by on a bike or skating down the path on rollerblades would take her for a surfer. Her own thin body, usually so cold, felt strengthened by the secure pressure of her wet suit. She waded out to her chest with the others and held tightly to her board. The group made an easy circle, with Rabbi Dovid at the center. Adina made certain not to look at anyone directly when they spoke, although she glanced sometimes at Anastasia, who was a mother and could have been a teacher or the woman at the bank, who had crashed her car with her children in the back seat, leaping onto the curb at eight in the morning into the clutch of arriving classmates who flew like startled birds. Miraculously, she had not killed anyone, but had broken both legs of the volunteer crossing guard. Anastasia called herself a "living amends" and was there by court order.

Adina had come to Beit T'Shuvah because her mother had begged her, had wrapped her arms around Adina's knees and sobbed. The truth was that even as she witnessed this, Adina felt nothing. Her father had taken her roughly by the arm, holding it up and away from her like a broken wing, and had guided her into the car. Adina had only observed them. She had taken Vicodin to sleep, but the coke was still in her system and she felt a clean kind of wholeness that did not belong to them. She was in the machine of her body and observed them only distantly, like the sound of a TV in a neighbor's apartment. She did not wish to consider that she was the source of the anguish that so distorted their faces, her mother's expression frantic, as if searching the sea for a child whose hand she had held a moment before, her father's face tightened by anger at Adina's weakness and at her mother's both. Anger at himself too, that he persisted in trying, having his own addiction to the promise of her return.

The following morning, in the tiny single bed at Beit T'Shuvah, Adina had felt a familiar pain, a pain that she believed lay in wait for her. It was the truth of her, a cold ache that she knew well. It was what made her different than her parents and her sister. She felt drawn in, at home, and a relentless beat of "this is who you are, this is the truth of you," spoke to her like a hollow sound. She felt not alone, but in the company of want. She was, she believed, in the presence of evil, and punished by a lifetime of restlessness. She was undeserving, she thought, of an ease that flowed through the world and eluded her. Those respites were untruths and the font of pain she felt now was the most true and forever. "God is love," she'd repeated, "God is love," shaping the words with her lips and in her mind. She had rocked herself under the thin blanket, aware of the blanketed shapes in her room of her roommates, unabashed, she spoke, her breath urgent and rhythmic, "God is love God is love God is love" she said, not knowing yet that this was her prayer.

As the sun rose and warmed the air around them, Rabbi Dovid led the group surrounding him in the water, in the prayer *Shehechianu*— a prayer of gratitude for having reached this day. Adina attended to each word as she said them, "*Shehechianu, V' keemanu, v'higianu laz-man hazeh.*" "That God gave us life and sustained us that we could reach this day." Others, she knew, had not. In the weeks since she had arrived at Beit T'Shuvah, many of their sessions were punctuated by an urgent Kaddish said for people who had come before her and who had failed; Leah, her roommate of two weeks, stealing a child's bicycle and riding to her dealer in Mar Vista so that she could use again, had been found in the cement stairwell of a grade school, the bike leaning up against a tree.

The group dispersed and, each with their own destination, headed into the surf. Rabbi Dovid looked out over the horizon and measured the waves. He felt the same as he did on the *bima* looking out on his congregation on Friday nights, buoyed by them—observing their grace and courage in the face of loss, watching as they navigated an uncertain future with hope and intention. They were the whole world and when he saw a child between two parents, he saw the cradle that sway between them. There, he saw the promise of family that gathers them up even in despair, even smarting from their own shame and wishing to push them away, to turn from them. Rabbi Dovid had seen Adina's father on Friday nights, lingering just outside the doorway, his body coiled with anger, unable, unwilling, to enter the sanctuary. Looking like a man with an appointment who had been kept waiting, he sometimes paced on the stairs on Venice Boulevard drawing in smoke from his cigarette and sharing the standing ashtray with Sol, who was both the receptionist and an addict. Sol had been promoted by Rabbi Dovid to answering the phones in his seventh month at Beit T'Shuvah. He had had accepted his position with pride and seriousness, although he didn't hear well because of a firecracker that was set off by malicious teenagers when he lay sleeping on the ground in the Nickel, that left him to only approximate the names of the callers, announcing, "A Mr. Rosensomething on line two." Sol smoked on the steps on his break from the phones. He wore slippers. Adina's father wore smart leather loafers, which he used to tamp out the cigarette before returning to the hall just outside the service.

When Adina gets up on the board and drops into the wave she feels she is a miracle. There is a rush of clean light through her body and she feels that she has a well of power. She rocks her weight and travels on the wave and she has a sense of new grace. For a moment she feels unbroken, she feels God. She wishes that she could never leave Beit T'Shuvah, because she suspects/knows that she will fail. She does not feel good in the world. She does not feel strong. She feels the disapproval of her father and that he is right about her, that what people say about her is true; that she is weak and that she is broken. That just as Tamara is whole and able, Adina is a burden and the source of her family's shame. A *shandeh* - that Simon Braverman's daughter is a drug addict. Adina thinks that it would be wise, best, to kill herself, and a plan forms. Then, she thinks it would be the best thing, the very best thing, to feel the coke in her body, to close her eyes and tilt her head back and be awash with bright clarity. And then she reminds herself that she is a child of God. That she is worthy of love. She hears the laughter of Anastatia as she maneuvers to stay up on her board. Adina addresses her *Yetser Ha'ra,* "I am stronger than you," she recites, "I have God and the matriarchs to drive you away, I have a higher power. I give myself over to a higher power." Adina finds her balance and, testing the strength in her body, rises again on the board. But for a moment she is distracted, she has thought about Efram, her dealer. She has imagined the return to what feels good right away, clean right away, and to be even, the correction that comes when her body is delicious with coke. She lists and smacks on the board and she is at once below the water, her face being driven into the tumbling rocks. She is alert to the push of the surf and reminds herself to relax her body. She knows that it is seconds, not moments, but she feels sure that she will die. She is tossed around and disoriented, the salt of the cold water in her nostrils and in her eyes. She fights the panic of her trapped heart and puts her hands ahead of her as she is not supposed to do, and badly scrapes her wrists. A rock strikes her shoulder. Then, she is standing, brought to her feet by Asher, who stands beside her still holding the heft of her arm. She comes to her feet and regards him. She feels helped. She looks at his clear green eyes and tousled brown hair, wet in curls framing his face. He is addicted to Vicodin and had a wife and a baby who left him. Adina ducks her head and wipes the salty cold water from her eyes with the back of her hand. Asher steps away, lifting his feet in what Adina sees now is shallow water, the sound of the waves crashing louder than her heartbeat. She sees that Rabbi Dovid watches her from a distance and she waves to him that she's okay. He observes her in the way that a mother might, craning her neck and shading her eyes against the sparkling water, finding her child, safe, flourishing. Adina wishes that she were a child and that she could begin each day with promise and possibility. She wishes that all of her were new again, and that she would enter the kitchen and her mother's eyes would reflect the bright future of each day instead of the fear that resided in her every look and gesture; Adina's past dragging behind her like a string of clattering cans.

Adina regarded the addicts around her and wondered which of them would recover, each with a family who would come tonight and pray with them, for them. Tamara had not come to Friday night services and Adina wondered, if she did, if she could even bear the weight of her sister's forgiveness. Tamara, who had judged her never, Tamara who after her parents had kicked her out had let Adina come to live with her in her small sunny apartment on Montana. Her year-older sister, who stood before her jewelry box, who had known what was missing and had said nothing, but had simply closed the small wooden drawer, accepting Adina's fragility as if it were her own shortcoming. Tamara, who comforted Adina by placing her whole body beside her and smoothing her hair, holding Adina as if she might be freezing, making Adina feel beloved. Every evening, Adina would go into her sister's unguarded wallet and remove, then later return, Tamara's ATM card, over the course of days bleeding the account of Tamara's savings, her tuition. Adina had used the money to buy drugs from up a guy from up north she sometimes partied with and had given him the key to her place so he could crash there. Tamara had awoken to the stranger standing over her bed, his hand rifling her purse.

Adina felt cold and floated out again into the water, her chest against the board, suddenly weary, as if she had clung to the board for days in the center of the ocean waiting for rescue. She let the water rock her and considered the other addicts as they moved through the water in her company. She felt a citizen of a country that was populated by people who were not fooled by her, had made her at once. "You are a liar," they might have said, " You are neither loyal or kind. Come and sit by me, Liar. This is your only home." Adina tried to imagine a future. She knew about herself that she was most able to fail. When she had been clean before, for sixty days or seventeen days or nine days, she had only ever felt that she was marking time, waiting patiently for the relief twinned with despair that was her only destination. If, for distracted moments, she did not think of or plan for her drug use, she felt accomplished. But then, like an author, she would construct her story with fresh detail, acquiring and discovering the cocaine, picturing herself first poised and then leaning back on the sofa of her dealer basking in the after, the undistracted brightness, the white noise of her drug.

The air was cool on her skin. She did not know if this time would be different, if she could assemble and gather the days after days until she was landed with firm feet into the next year, if her name would appear in the newsletter beside the week's Torah potion to mark her year drug-free. Rabbi Dovid looked at her as you would a child who had fallen, his eyes a steady bridge to standing. She saw also that he was running a swift calculation, and would sometimes look away to conceal it from her. She had been cautioned by Rabbi Dovid that he could not draw them forward on this journey, but only hold the light to make clear their path. In the shadow cast by his lantern, she discerned his own fear for her. They might advance together through a dark cavern and she nearly always wished to announce herself unable to do the hard work of living in a life so described by shame, so measured in failure. Adina was lulled by the waves that rocked the board she clung to. Rabbi Dovid tucked his own board under his arm and signaled with a wave of his arm that is was time to come in.

Toweling off their hair and breathing with vigor, the group prepared for *Shacharit*, the morning prayer. Asher unzipped the duffle that contained the prayer books and distributed them to the others. Anastasia, with motherly care, removed the *tallisim* and passed them around beginning with Adina. Before Beit T'Shuvah, Adina had never worn a *tallis*. She was hardly religious and did not think of herself as much of a Jew. She was just as familiar with Christmas in her own home, where they had a catered party every year for the holiday with people from her father's agency. They did not light a menorah; she was not sure they even owned one, though she thought she might have seen one tucked into a cabinet with rarely used objects; the waffle iron, the electric knife. When Adina was younger, she had been to Bat Mitzvahs of girls in her class, but had only ever talked through the service, sitting in a far back row with her girlfriends. She had felt like an imposter when she had first arrived at Beit T'Shuvah, but they had put her at ease, Rabbi Dovid teaching her the melodies and the meaning of the prayers, as if it had all been there waiting for her. She liked holding the prayer book, which even before she understand the words in it, had comforted her. She began to sleep with it in her hands, to carry it with her finger marking a page that said *"Hineeni*—Here I am, Behold me of little merit trembling and afraid, I stand before you." This was how they answered at morning meeting when they took roll. 'Adina Braverman, addict, Hineeni. Here I am."

Rabbi Dovid regarded the congregation that stood before him. He summoned his brother to his side, as he did every day at the start of his prayer. He was aware keenly of the way in which he had failed him. He admonished himself for the thought and remembered the service led by Rabbi Snow for Eytan. The room was filled with people who loved him, but their love had not filled him. Dovid's love had not filled him. He remembered him as they had been lying under the stars at Joshua Tree, the rocks beneath them still warm with the day's sun. "I don't know how," Eytan had said. Dovid had rocked up on an elbow to hear the rest of what his brother had to say. But he had said nothing more. And Dovid had only lain back down and watched the stars burn and drop from the black felt sky.

Adina took the corners of the *tallis* and drew it around herself. Rabbi Dovid had taught them that the *tallis* was a reminder of the 613 commandments in the Torah, a number so daunting as to reassure her. She could "do the next indicated thing" six hundred and thirteen times and perhaps the tasks would occupy her, carry her to a new place. The cloth with knotted strands was an instructive tool to be worn in the daylight. Rabbi Dovid had read from Psalm 104 "God covered himself with light as a garment who drew the heavens out like a curtain," and Adina imagined the *tallis* as the whole blue sky. Adina held the *tallis* around her and brought her hands together at the wrists, making a silent illuminated tent. This was her time to make a vow, a dedication for her prayer, and she prayed that she know how to live. That could accomplish her t'shuva, and return to the world. The sun filled the space she had made with white sun and the air through the taut fabric shivered.

Shlosha

ON THE THIRD DAY of mourning, Ayelet Halpern went to Gelson's. There wasn't anything she needed; the double refrigerators were filled to the top with trays from Canter's and Barney Greengrass. Ayelet had spent the three days of Shiva on a low chair, an apricot rugelach tucked into a napkin clutched in her hand like a talisman. The house was filled with people on the first and second days, so many after the funeral that a valet was hired; suit jackets tossed across the guest room bed like a party. This morning the minyan had come from the men's club at the temple, writers mostly who left after the morning prayers and headed for Starbucks with their laptops. Uncovering the mirror in the foyer, Ayelet told them she was fine and thank you and they didn't need to return. Josh Stern, whose son Jake had gone to preschool with Hannah and Emma at Beth Shalom, stood at Ayelet's doorway and stepped back toward her as if he had to make a correction, *just one more thing*, but as he began to speak he thought better of it and bar mitzvah-kissed her on the cheek instead, his skin warm and clean and comforting in a way that surprised her. He had lost his own mother in the fall.

When they had gone, Ayelet stood at the open door of the refrigerator and drew the trash can from under the sink over beside her. One by one she threw out the containers of coleslaw, the potato salad, a quart of mustard, and perhaps two dozen assorted sandwiches—pastrami, turkey, corned beef, each cut in half and held together with a frilly toothpick. She knew what she was doing was a sin, to waste food, that she could have easily delivered it to a food pantry or to the fire station near her house, but what she also knew was that she could not look at the food on the trays even one minute longer. When she had filled the second plastic bagful, she hooked the red drawstring with her finger and carried the bags to the trash herself without waiting for her husband to return from work. She rocked back the lid on the huge can and swung the bags in. She closed the top again and felt the satisfaction of the sound when it shut. Back in her kitchen, she washed her hands with lavender antibacterial soap. With a paper towel and warm water, she wiped down the now-empty shelves of her bright Sub Zero, closed the door and located her keys, so she could drive down the hill to the store. Her mother had been dead for just over seventy-two hours.

Ayelet Halperin was born in Los Angeles, a native, people made a fuss over it when she was out to dinner with her husband, "Really, you're from here?" as if that made her less than. She would point out that she had gone to law school at Columbia where she had met Ryan; nevertheless, they would regard her as if she had grown up in a sitcom. Ayelet's mother Stella had moved to Toluca Lake from Cleveland in '58 and she and Ayelet's father Abe had been inbetweeners for Warner Bros. Ayelet was three when her father died and could not summon memories of him that had not been recited to her. She struggled sometimes to find a true image of him, but all were populated by the black and white photographs that her mother had ordered in albums, the oldest ones framed with black corners like arrowheads. As a girl she would lay across the chenille bedspread in her mother's room and invite herself to their wedding: her father strong and compact, his hand around her mother's delicate waist, a look between them so direct you knew they had slept together.

Stella had worked at Warner Bros. until she retired in 1980 and after just a month at home had returned as a docent at the museum on the lot. Until her diagnosis, Stella spent every Wednesday and Friday giving tours upstairs of the original props from *Harry Potter*. She would work the secret mic on the sorting hat and put children, as she assessed them, into Slytherin or Gryffindor, rarely Hufflepuff. In October on a faculty day, Ayelet had taken the twins to see their grandmother and at lunch in the commissary, Stella had called over John Stamos.

Dressed in a Juicy sweat suit, Ayelet used Windex and a paper towel to remove the foggy coating on the mirror in her bathroom that had been sprayed on using a can provided by Forest Lawn. As she emerged in the reflection she noticed she looked worn and tired and was grateful she had had her lashes tinted before the funeral so that she had not run her face with mascara like a Lichtenstein painting. She did not dwell on the image of herself, but averted her eyes as she might if she had encountered an estranged friend with whom she wasn't reconciled. Ayelet sat on the edge of the bed and rocked her heel into her Asics walking shoes, flipped off the light and, crossing the room, removed the iPod from the dock, silencing the song by her neighbor k.d. lang.

Backing out the Lexus, things felt right again. Watching the gate close reliably behind her, Ayelet looked back at the lovely home, at the Mexican sage that had gotten so full this year, then directed her car down Laurel Canyon to her grocery store. She would have plenty of time to do the shopping and grab a coffee at Peet's before she picked up the girls from Campbell Hall.

Rabbi Snow had done the service for her mother. Stella had told her explicitly that it was not to be the young female rabbi, whom Stella scandalously called Rabbi Gidget. Stella was braver than Ayelet, had had to be. Ayelet gripped the wheel tighter thinking of her. She would pick up some Chinois chicken salads for the girls. Hannah favored Stella with her dark eyes and Emma was fair like Ryan's family. And number 4 coffee filters.

At Gelson's, Ayelet loaded her cart, beginning with skirt steak that she would marinate for dinner and then California rolls with smelt eggs for Hannah who liked them after school. Hannah, who seemed hungry all the time, had outstripped her twin by two inches last checkup. Hannah could be unkind to Emma in ways Ayelet could not invent, and Ayelet would sometimes favor Emma as a form of protection, breaking the rule of twin fairness by letting Emma have special time with her, sitting on the edge of the sink letting her try on blush while Hannah worked at the kitchen counter excelling. Emma, who exhausted herself for B's but was all grace and love and drew friends to herself effortlessly the way half a dozen butterflies had alighted on her last summer at the Natural History museum. Ayelet was rounding to the coffee filter aisle when her phone rang. "Hey, Sweetpea," she answered when she read that the source of the call was Emma. Emma's voice was quiet, as if her head were tucked in. She asked Ayelet to come get her with not even forty-five minutes until pickup. Ayelet abandoned the cart in the aisle and was already tweetsing the alarm on the car before Emma asked a second time, "Can you come now?"

The phone connection was still open, Emma only closing the phone when she could see her mother's car. Ayelet parked under the looming eucalyptus trees in the school lot and Emma moved toward her, her hoodie tied around her waist. Ayelet closed the gap between them in five strides and knew at once why she had called. Emma placed her body next to her mother's and Ayelet lifted Emma's chin to address her, tracing the curve of her bangs and tucked them behind her ear. "Did you have something with you?" Emma nodded. Ayelet had made a kit for both girls at the start of the year—what looked like an anime pencil case with tampon, minipad, clean panties, and Tylenol. Ayelet had not predicted that Emma would be first. Hannah appeared minutes later, striding across the lot in her basketball shorts, annoyed at being interrupted, "What?" Emma looked at her mother pleadingly and Ayelet protected her. "Orthodontist's. Can you get a ride with Cali?" Hannah regarded them as if she could not know how she was related to either of them. "Yeah." She took the path back to PE in loping strides. Ayelet wished she had the California rolls to give Hannah and felt somehow guilty and found out for being without them.

Alone in the car, Emma repeated the story of her discovery to her mother, more animated than she had been before. When Ayelet had gotten her period she had been at home in the yellow house with her mother and she had called out to her from the only bathroom in their home. Stella had shown her how to secure a pad to her panties and had called her best friend Phyllis and the three of them had gone over the hill to Mr. Chow's for Chinese food. Ayelet flipped her phone to dial her mother and in the space of the ring shut the phone before the message picked up. She glanced quickly at Emma, relived that she had not observed her making the call. At home she made some noodle soup for Emma and microwave popcorn and they watched a TiVo-ed Scrubs together on the sofa, a blanket across both their laps. When Hannah returned home after school she slammed her heavy pile of books on the counter and opened the fridge. "There's nothing to eat," she said to neither one of them.

In the morning before Ayelet's eyes opened to the light-filled room, she forgot utterly that her mother had died and was shocked and newly angry when she opened them. She showered quickly and made her way down to the kitchen. She pulled on her Asics, hoping to resume her 3.3 mile daily walk on Mulholland, when she remembered that both girls needed to be actually seen by the orthodontist in Tarzana. She sat in the waiting area and read Redbook and Good Housekeeping, flipping through articles on cancer detection and recipes for cake. When she had dropped the girls at school, she drove over the hill to Soolip to order response cards for the condolence cards that were collecting un-opened on the table in a basket in the dining room. Afterward she stopped at Joan's on Third, where she saw her rabbi on line ahead of her buying a baguette and olive oil. Seeing her, Ayelet left behind the lovely orange blossom scented marshmallows she had selected for Emma and once again felt in trouble and found out.

Ayelet drove back over Laurel Canyon to pick up the girls and drive them to the Westside for a basketball game at Crossroads. They sat in the back seat with a distance between them that they extended by molecules. Hannah was sullen and stormy, telling Emma to "Stop it" and "Cut it out" in full fury from a standing start. Emma drew herself up and canted her body away from the displeased Hannah, letting her long bangs fall in a curtain between them. On the court, they seemed to briefly forget they were sisters. Ayelet and Ryan, careful always to give them separate lives, had not found a way to split basketball. But it had turned out not to be a worry: the girls, in the swift intensity of the game, trained their eyes on each other as teammates. Better matched on the court than on other playing fields, Emma lithe and focused, Hannah forceful and sure, together they bounded down the court as experts, teammates, friends. Ayelet hoped to herself that she could remember to step out of the way of them. When their fighting would become intolerable, Ayelet sometimes played her trump card, that she would not live forever, that they would have only each other. "It will be Emma," she would predict, "who you will call when your heart is broken." She only hoped that Emma, in her natural beauty and ease, was not also the cause. They were good girls and she was proud of them—the best thing she had done. Hannah and Emma pounded down the court after the same loose ball, the loud squeak of their shoes punctuated by a shrill whistle. Hannah fell out of bounds and nearly into the folding chairs that edged the court, landing on her extended wrist. She drew her arm into herself and, looking past the coach, glared at Emma, who reared back and raised her hands instinctively. The coach placed her body between them and, instructing Hannah to walk it off, blew the whistle to resume play. Hannah watched after her sister, younger by eight minutes, as she flew down the court flaunting a new confidence, leaving her behind. She knows, Ayelet realized belatedly, of course, she knows.

The following evening, Ayelet dressed in an Armani sheath of grey wool. She had gotten it at Neiman's and it was a classic. She stepped into her Prada heels and ducked her head into the pearls that Ryan had gotten her when he moved back in after the affair. It had happened early in their marriage when the girls were not yet three. Ayelet had traded her sweats for a Philippe Adec suit she had from when she was still working. It had been an effort to fasten the skirt, but still, returning to the office where they had once worked together, she had felt pretty. When the new associate stepped into Ryan's office, Ayelet knew at once that she was sleeping with her husband. She had entered the room and framed herself beside him as if they were in a portrait together. Ayelet was incredulous, not at the fact of the affair but that no one was speaking of it. She wanted to throw up, but more she wanted someone to say out loud what was so plain to her. The play-acting of the next several moments infuriated her; the young associate asking to see pictures of the twins, as if she didn't know. Later at home, when Ayelet had confronted Ryan, he had cried like a girl, wanting to be held and forgiven—his dilemma so tragic and conflicted that for four weeks he had taken a month to month rental at the Oakwood Apartments, which were populated by child actors and their mothers who would decamp after pilot season. Ayelet's mother had purchased a pecan alligator from Victor Benes and, while the twins slept on the matching sofas nearby, told Ayelet that the choice was hers, that she would love her no less if she abandoned or returned to her marriage. She told her that he, Ryan, was not her concern, that she was a mother to Ayelet only and Bubbe to the girls. But she couldn't help adding that Ryan had never been as smart as Ayelet. When Ayelet decided to remain with Ryan, so that the girls might have their father, Stella had remained true to her word and never again referred to it. He returned home conditionally and after a month's time in the guesthouse, Ayelet had asked Ryan to come back into the house, her body betraying her by longing for him. Standing now, in front of the mirror, Ayelet tested her hair up and then down the way Ryan liked it. When he stepped into their shared bedroom she found him handsome. At his request, she had sprayed perfume on her wrist and at the delicate scoop of her neck and, where once it would have transported her, the hint of vanilla and notes of amber tonight gave her a headache.

Ayelet kissed the girls goodnight, patting Emma's hand on her way out. She lay her clutch on the seat beside Ryan as he drove. They met David Kessler and his wife at Jar. The chef, Suzanne, whose son had gone to preschool with the twins, came out of the kitchen and lingered at their table. When Ryan placed the order for dinner, Suzanne leaned into her and in the over-live dining room told Ayelet that she was so sorry to hear about her mother. Suzanne had lost her father the spring before and Ayelet had read about it in the Temple newsletter. Ayelet let the men talk emphatically while she sipped the Stag's Leap the sommelier had suggested. After one sip it made her wish to be at home with the girls on either side of her. She felt that the room full of diners were altogether strangers to her. Mayor Villaraigosa sat in the booth in the corner with a woman who could only be his wife, so strongly did she resemble the reporter he had left her for. Ayelet sat back in the tall chair, her exposed arms cool but lovely to her husband, who eyed her over the rim of his raised glass. She smiled back at him and let the walla of the restaurant wash over her and relied on the artifice of her slender body to hold court while she wished herself away.

When they returned home that evening, the girls sat at the kitchen counter together eating raw cookie dough in a truce of habit that came from having always shared the world. Ayelet wished to remain with them, but kissed their heads in a huddle and followed her husband up to bed. Ayelet allowed herself to keep her eyes closed and herself quiet as her husband made love to her. Afterward, she drew herself to the side of the bed and made a sleepy hum of appreciation, so that he would believe he had lulled her. The wine, at least, had hastened her sleep.

Ryan, basking in the good will that follows marital sex, had offered to drop the girls for her, leaving Ayelet momentary unanchored—the girls once again drawing away from her when she had wanted most to be near them. The kitchen air wafting with the enticing smell of the toaster waffles as they threw their backpacks into the trunk of her husband's black BMW, as empty and new as it had been in the showroom. She watched them pull out of the drive, Hannah leaning forward from the back seat to change the radio station, Emma applying gloss to her lips in the folded down visor, Ryan as happy as she had ever seen him. Ayelet hurried through a yogurt while standing and, taking only her keys and her phone in her pockets, pulled the door to the house closed behind her and began her walk around the block.

Ayelet tucked her arms to her sides and her hands into the pockets of her sweatshirt. She would be warm in a minute, but for now she felt the chill in the air—that in Southern California always seemed like a misunderstanding—slip into the back of her neck. She quickened her pace, hoping to warm herself. She was, she had noticed lately, cold all the time and thought this must mean her estrogen was dropping which seemed to account for everything. She had made this walk a hundred times, more, starting after she had given birth to the twins, getting her body back in months, feeling the relief of the open space, the view of the otherwise unbeautiful valley. She would make the loop and knew by now when to cross so that she could be seen on the blind corners, reassured by the reliable appearance of the handsome young firemen from the station on Mulholland who would lap her twice while running and who she had to admit now seemed like boys to her.

The air was cool and the ground wet from what must have been a brief early morning rain. Ayelet always felt grateful for what was winter in Los Angeles, the New Yorkers at the firm where she had worked with her husband always doubting it. Not so emphatic as the school-closing snow of back east, but the changes to her beautiful and subtle. She rubbed her shoulders and quickened her pace to break through the chill. The whole day in front of her, only a trip back to the grocery store and a doctor's appointment to schedule for Emma; all her tasks, she realized, could now be accomplished by someone found on Craig's List. The girls lapping her also—in two years driving, in four going off to college. She wondered if she could go back to work now if she wanted to; many of her friends instead becoming, in the shelter of their husband's income, painters and daily practicers of yoga. The sound of a car rounding the corner caught Ayelet's attention and looking up, she was rewarded with an arbor of entwined bougainvillea and morning glory, fuchsia and indigo. She was smart still, she knew, but not current. She didn't even know, she admitted, what the minimums for a script were. But she could learn again if she wanted to. She paused on the shoulder, then turned down Woodrow Wilson into the neighborhoods, the whine of a saw and the rhythmic hammering of a Neutra being remodeled echoing through the canyon. The sun was warming the wet streets, steam rising off the surface. She unzipped her jacket and, shaking it off while still walking, she tied it around her waist, her footfall closer to a run as she came to the lowest part of the loop, her heart pounding at the rise. She dug into the steps of the incline. Her mother was dead. Ayelet insisted that her feet continue. Her mother was dead. Ayelet drew in a shock of air. She felt the curve of the entire world and, as if her heart took flight, she made a frantic search of the round world for her mother. Her arms fell to her side and the trees above her seemed stunningly tall; the sky above them bright and far. She noticed that her feet were not advancing and thought, were it not for the tacky surface of her shoes, she might fall. Her mother was not here. Ayelet ran a quick inventory and located her beloved daughters. They were there at school: Hannah, her books clutched in front of her chest, and Emma, the sun on her hair, the sound of her laughter a guide to her. Ayelet's winged heart located them and flew back to her body. Only them. Not the man she had stayed married to for them. He was, she knew at once, not her real husband. Not someone to whom she owed anything. Her mother had been right, although she had not said a word. Stella, who was her only mother, was silent in this new world that was utterly without her. Ayelet stood on the street and could not walk a step further. She lowered herself to a felled redwood branch and sat, on this, the seventh day of her mother's Shiva.

Shidach

IRA BERGER GOT THERE FIRST. He found a table in the far corner of Mozza and sat there for a full fifteen minutes before she walked in. Being late was something he hated. People who let themselves be late indulged themselves while the world turned. He felt the same way about people who left trash in their cars, like they were preparing to live out of it if suddenly snowbound in LA. He had gotten the reservation by putting an alert on his laptop that reminded him to call on a Thursday for a table in four weeks on a Sunday and he had done it and, though he doubted very much that the young widow would care about it, he cared about it, was proud of it—the way he felt about his on-time taxes and tidy car, the way he felt about light bulbs that were changed and batteries that were at the ready. The door flung open and she stood there, rifling her purse, squinting. He had plenty of time to observe her as she located what turned out to be her glasses and, now seeing, gave the hostess her name. He stood at his seat and, as the hostess pointed at him he simultaneously discerned the napkin on his lap was attached by static. She made her way across the room, waving her arm vigorously as if greeting a relative at Ellis Island. He disengaged the napkin from his lap and leaning his hand on the table shattered a breadstick that sprayed shards of bread all over his pants. She had closed the gap more quickly than he had expected and extended her hand to his that had just been brushing his crotch and for this he hated her already.

Iris Tellerman was late. She had lingered too long in the mirror of her bathroom looking at her recently dyed eyebrows. They were too dark—as if tinted by Sharpie—and although Melora had assured her they would fade to normal in several days, she did not have several days and decided that she would rub them down with baking soda and peroxide toothpaste to fade them. This method had been, actually, somewhat effective and had left a satisfying smudge on the white washcloth. She had gotten the same toothpaste on the left breast of the only dress she felt comfortable in and her attempts to remove the swath of white had left a spreading stain that reminded her of her breastfeeding days. She had pulled the dress over her shoulders and redressed herself in a skirt and sweater that was neither attractive nor comfortable but was mostly clean and she had no reason to please this man just because his mother knew her mother from the temple. The sitter had come with fuchsia bangs that delighted Vered. The tail of a tattooed carp swished out from under the sleeve of the sitter's t-shirt. Iris thought twice, but left her the uncomplicated recipe for mac and cheese and left. She'd walked the three blocks to Mozza (her neighborhood suddenly cool) not to be green, but to transition; it was so long since she had dated. She tried to sit down. Ira belatedly pulled out the chair for her and there was some difficulty with her purse, which was slung across her body and had been buttoned somehow under her sweater. Ira stood waiting as she disentangled herself, which frankly made her feel scrutinized. She deposited the purse on the third of four chairs of their table and rebuttoning her sweater, pulled her seat forward and said hello to this man her whose name annoyingly rhymed with hers.

IRA HAD GONE to the trouble of ordering appetizers so he wouldn't starve to death while he waited for her and, within moments of sitting down, fried squash blossoms arrived in front of her. She oohed in surprise like a girl and people from the next table turned to the sound. She had leaned forward and patted him on the top of his sleeve, which gave him a surprise jolt in his body. She was pretty, he acknowledged, in a New York-editor kind of way—the intelligence hard to deny, her hair a rich brown, with eyebrows he could only describe as fierce. At the corner of her dark eyes the story of her losses were described in thin lines. Ira had taken his mother, who lived at Park La Brea for their weekly trip to Ralphs for groceries when she'd asked him. He'd opened the car door and offered his arm for his mother to brace herself—surprised each time by the cool softness of her flesh, not the batter's arms he had eluded in his youth. When he had come around and placed himself in the driver's seat he had sensed her waiting in the way that she did when she was preparing to manipulate him, which he let her do as if in agreement. It was then that she mentioned Iris—Rose and Jer's daughter—widowed, with children. Ira allowed his mother two of these *shidachs* a year, because he had no wish to cause her distress. The women were always smart and accomplished with a vague eagerness to please. The last had been a concert violinist with a law degree, but he had no interest in her or the others, did not even attempt to sleep with them though all had made it plain that he could. He was never unkind, but neither was he interested. Dating only a pretense for him, a patient biding of time, because Ira Berger was in love with his wife.

His wife, Marla, his *beshert*, who had just had a child with Jeffrey, a man Ira would kill in his sleep were it not for the anger that would certainly inspire in her. This way he continued to have access to her, short bursts of time when he dropped off and collected their daughter, Maya. Ira would linger just inside the door of the Hancock Park home they once shared and he could feel on his flesh if Jeffrey were in the house or not. If he were, Ira would speak to Marla in almost a whisper, making romantic the most mundane, planning with his delicate bride for parent-teacher conferences or following up on their shared meeting with Maya's therapist in Century City. Ira was still grateful to be in the same space with her and to breathe her, like a cat sipping milk-breath from an infant. That she went to bed each night with a man who was not him, that that man's hand reached under her Hanro nightgown for her teacup of a breast, even placed his mouth over the rosy nipple distressed Ira, but did not discourage him. He understood, in what he could only name in his soul, that this woman who leaned on the banister in her white t-shirt and sweats was his. When she called up the stairs to Maya he observed the cleft in her neck where dew would gather if she were to sleep all night in the grass. He had fractured a glass with all his strength in the presence of witnesses and this Jeff, this interloper, was nothing to him.

IRA AND IRIS sat without speaking for a moment, the clatter and din of the restaurant a substitute for conversation—the table beside them too lively with a group of women celebrating a birthday; their laughter loud even in a loud room. They were passing around scandalous panties as favors.

"How old are your kids?" Ira ventured. Iris was burning her fingertips on the *arancini*, the stuffed rice ball she nibbled on. She placed the half-eaten appetizer back on the plate and patted her lips with the napkin. Setting it back on her lap, she regarded him before answering, made a brief study of him, and then she spoke gazing down, about her children, suddenly beautiful. As she began, Ira realized, he had only been making conversation and did not want to know, alarmed to have taken this step toward her. He regretted that he pictured them: the boy, nine, fair as his father had been and the girl, just seven, dark like her mother. He felt a pang and, without wanting to, began to mentally organize his household to include them, like a girl in Junior High testing a boy's last name on the back of a spiral notebook. Involuntarily, he pictured Maya helping the little girl with her homework. Then, with the effort of doing calculus, he pushed the image from his mind.

At least the food is good, thought Iris, who now used a fork to draw the melted mozzarella from the center of the delicious treat. She had agreed to go on the date under pressure from Melora and her mother. Her mother portrayed her hesitation as selfish—as if each day she didn't date she deprived her children of a father. She had raised the subject at Shabbat in front of the children. Iris had only just pinched the salty skin of the chicken and was about to lay it on her tongue when Rose brought it up. Both children bowed their heads as if in an involuntary grace. Iris had agreed mostly to end the description of him: divorced, a lawyer—insulted at the criteria that Jewish was enough. She knew from Melora that Ira's wife had left him for a co-worker, and she did not wish to hear this again. She had heard her mother depict other such *shandehs* sitting at the kitchen table spooling the thread of the Red Rose teabag and pressing the last drops of tea from the bag against the spoon.

Iris took a moment to study Ira, whose hands she noticed, were meticulously groomed, as was the rest of him—his hair looking as if it were cut daily, the beds of his nails buffed pink. She tested herself for a sexual attraction and was surprised to find a kind of hum in her body, as if she had developed a sudden fetish for lawyers. She felt briefly proud of herself for her light yearning, relieved that her body was leading her against her own fear and resistance. She had expressed her anger earlier this evening to her deceased husband, who had left her so exposed, telling him on the way over that it was his fault she had to go on this date and that whatever came of it was on his head. But she felt utterly safe from acting, the mere thought of the *shidach* and the assembled parents at their bedside rooting them on a certain cure for the attraction.

"Your daughter's fifteen?" she offered. "She is." He shook his head and a smile crossed his face as in memory. "Hard to believe." Then, "she's driving now." "Are you teaching her?" "Driving?" Ira laughed. "No, I wouldn't survive it, her stepfather's teaching her." As he said the words, Iris saw a flash of planning that she could only describe as homicidal.

OVER A GLASS of Shafer merlot, Iris and Ira discussed the Woody Allen movie they had both seen, which Iris declared a misogynist fantasy, *Entourage*—porn you can Tivo; the TV show *Dexter*, a weekly dose of evil, saying she would rather watch a rerun of *Gilmore Girls* or *The Sisterhood of the Traveling Pants*. "Happiness," she posited, "is not less authentic than unhappiness." They discovered they had both once volunteered on the same Big Sunday project at the Breed Street Shul. They agreed that education was wanting, that mental illness should be de-stigmatized, and that LA billboards were egregious. Their pizzas arrived—hers with Gorgonzola dolce, fingerling potatoes, radicchio & rosemary; his with tomato, rapini & *burrata*. Iris's phone rang.

She half-stood and reached across the pizzas to reclaim her bag, which rang like the weighted phone of a desk sergeant. Her sweater draped into the food and Ira made an effort to assist her without groping her, finally grabbing the bag instead and holding it while she peered inside for the ringing phone. She removed the phone and left him with the purse in midair, which he continued to hold as he lowered himself to his seat. He considered the pizza in front of him, but waited as she completed her call. "Let me talk to her." Iris said and rose to grab her bag. "You're okay, baby, I'll be right there." She folded the phone and replaced it in her purse. "I have to go," said Iris, "My little girl's sick." "I'm sorry," Ira extended her purse to her as he rose. She looked at him impatiently. "You have to drive me. I walked," she said as if he should know this. Ira extracted four twenties and signaled the waiter for the check. "Here," he said, and gave the valet ticket to Iris, who went ahead of him out the door.

IRA'S PRIUS ARRIVED. It was then she saw the wire entrails sprouting from the neck of the mirror where she had sheared it off. She regarded it, alarmed, then, remembering the waiting valet, walked around to the passenger side and tucked herself into the seat. Ira arrived a moment later with the two pizza's boxed and still warm and handed them across to Iris, who rested them on her knees. She looked over at Ira as she drew her seatbelt across her body and said nothing as he pulled out into the traffic on Highland. "They didn't even leave a note," Ira said, his neck craning to make up the vista compromised by the absent mirror. "But I did," Iris thought, and remembered in detail writing the words on the back of a lunch menu from Vered's school. Iris wondered what this could mean. She knew the Jewish lore of couples being *beshert*. She had believed that about her own husband and their children were certainly proof of that but then he had died. She found it hard to believe that she was intended to be a widow and then later intended to be with Ira, as if the world had a new script each day; first green, then goldenrod, then pink pages. There were a lot of Priuses in LA and she was pretty sure she didn't even like Ira. He made a left onto Melrose and five minutes later Iris was home.

Ira pulled into the driveway and Iris bounded out of the car. "Thanks," she said and hopped out, heading quickly inside. She had placed the pizzas on the dash and he watched after her as she disappeared into the house, the door left ajar, the lights of the living room gold against the dark. Then he saw her purse in the well where she had left it. Ira pressed the button that turned off the car. Taking the pizza boxes in one hand and the purse in the other, he walked across the front lawn to the house. As he approached the door the babysitter exited and he caught the screen door with his free hand. A pajama'd boy stood at the end of the long hall, holding a wet washcloth. He walked past Ira and regarded him only casually as he walked to the living room, where Iris kneeled beside Vered. The child wore a pink nightgown— the kind his own daughter wore at that age—her feet in white ankle socks that had been walked around in. As Iris took the washcloth from her son—Ira remembered as if he had always known it that the boy's name was Evan—she drew the cool cloth across Vered's forehead, leaving behind damp curls. She took the washcloth and holding one hand and then the other wiped them. "There you go, better." Iris slipped her arms below the child and came to standing. As she turned, she saw Ira at the door, holding the pizza and her purse. The child let her head fall against her mother's shoulder. "Thanks," she said, using her head to indicate where to set it down. She walked down the hall to the child's bedroom and the boy followed, pulling the door closed behind. Ira walked across the empty living room and placed the purse on the dining room chair, a plastic laundry basket occupied the other chair filled with unmatched socks. The table was littered with schoolwork—the beginnings of a diorama depicting a California mission. The boy appeared in the kitchen with the little girl's blankets, and lifting the white lid of the washer dropped them in and without speaking he left the kitchen. Ira took the pizza boxes and placed them on the counter in the kitchen. Brightly colored dishes lay in the drain and others lay unwashed in the sink. On the sill above the sink, sat a glass jar with a pencil across the top with a white string tied around falling into the water forming sugar crystals. Ira turned the faucet to the right and filled the tub. He unbuttoned first his left cuff and rolled the sleeve, then repeated the action on his right. He plunged the sponge into the hot soapy water and made quick work of the dishes, before turning his attention to the socks in the bin. Finding for each, a match, and bringing the pair together at the top, tucking one neatly into the other.

The Heart of a Stranger

ALISON EMORY ROSENBLATT carried the cellophane wrapped *Mad Men* gift basket up the stairs of the temple. Inside was a script from the episode signed by the cast, a *Mad Men* baseball jacket, and a signed eight by ten of Jon Hamm, whose agent was Jewish and rode the stationary bike next to Alison at Spinning class. Alison knew that this basket would bring in a large donation, not as large as the walk-on appearance on *Entourage*, but more than the gift certificate for life coaching or the introductory class at Pilates Silver Lake. She had left the basket on the counter in the kitchen this morning so that Seth would see it. She busied herself with Hannah's lunch so that she would be looking away when he noticed it. And he did notice it, and she briefly swelled with pride that he was aware of her successes at the temple, that he was pleased with her role there, as he had been when she made latkes on Chanukah or served hot lunch at the Day School. She was exhausted from Co-chairing the silent auction—which she did with Tamara Weiss, for whom being Jewish was as easy as waking up—but it was worth it for the times that Seth beamed at her and slipped his hand to the small of her back and kissed her on her hair, which was the color of the corn silk in the fields she road her bike past in her Iowa summers.

At the top of the stairs she encountered Rabbi Beth, who seemed more beautiful than usual if that were possible. Sophie resembled the rabbi more than she did Alison and emulated her the way that she once had a Disney princess, recently asking for a shiny black raincoat that she had seen the rabbi wearing on a rare California day of rain. Rabbi Beth smiled broadly at Alison. She was escorting a tall man whose tilted-down head shaded his eyes; when he lifted his head Alison saw they were a startling blue. Rabbi Beth began to introduce them but, shifting the large basket, Alison could still only offer two fingers. "I converted Alison," she offered to the man she had introduced as Dev something, the sounds obscured by the crinkling package. "Brennen," he repeated. Alison nodded realizing that he must be converting as well. She felt at once a cousin to him and shifted the package to watch him descend the stairs with Rabbi Beth. Beth was speaking quietly and he listening intently. Alison felt a pang of something and had the impulse to set down the basket and go after him and say…what? She righted the basket and made her way to the boardroom, where the swag for the Purim Carnival was being stored.

The women were dishing about the smoking hot new cantor. "It would help if he could be a little less handsome," said Tamara, (who had recently volunteered for the choir) to Leah Kaplan, who had brought in dinner for two at Jar and party for five at Color Me Mine. The new cantor was handsome; Alison noticed that at this temple in LA the spiritual leaders were all somewhat beautiful. Even Rabbi Snow, with the crinkles at his eyes, was handsome in a boyish way. She had felt the same when she had done jury duty in Beverly Hills: the bailiff a fit African-American, the court stenographer a bright Latina, the judge too looking as if he had been cast. Alison was keenly aware of the way in which she was cast in the role of non-Jewish wife—the *blunde shisksa*—as she had heard herself described by her mother-in-law on the phone. Tamara held Alison's basket overhead and admired it. Leah Kaplan nibbled a cookie left from this morning's Board meeting. "Niiice," she said approvingly. Leah Kaplan had been in Alison's B'nai Mitzvah class, Alison surprised at what Leah didn't know. Alison, who had approached her conversion with intention, had the deeper knowledge of an outsider, the way that Latina nannies in LA must master American history to become citizens. The truth was that Seth had only the most superficial knowledge of his own faith. When she had provided the explanation of the laws concerning *shiva* he had admonished her. She had been hurt in the moment, but in the moment after, he had pulled her yet closer and she let her anger fall away. Still, at Passover at his parent's house when Sophia asked the four questions, Alison had kept the answers to herself. Alison had agreed to convert for Seth's grandmother Bubbe Sara. Seth had taken Alison to his grandmother's apartment on West 81st when they had been dating only a few weeks. He was lighthearted and teasing, but she had been terrified. When she set foot in the apartment she bit her own lip against the welling tears. She loved Seth in a way that made her frightened. She had no restraint for her feelings and had wanted to marry him from before the first time they had slept together. They had seen *Diva* at the Aero on Broadway and he had kissed her outside of the theatre in the snow. He had tucked her hands into his warm coat pockets and with his hands he had held her face. When he drew her into the apartment of his Bubbe Sara, she felt terrified that she might fail a test. His Bubbe, who was small and feeding a turquoise bird, told Alison that in the old country a prospective bride was given a chain to untangle and that was the measure of her patience. Alison had offered her hands, expecting the test, and Sara had taken them in hers instead, declaring her "a good girl" and a "*shayna punim*," and asking her to reach the Maxwell House coffee down from a high shelf.

Alison had wished that Sara had lived to meet Sophie. She had been pregnant and was eating barley soup that Sara had made for her when Seth received the call that she had died. Alison had wept and wept. The baby, born a month later, was named for her. The bird, Zuz, was theirs now, still in the kitchen in an open cage. Seth's mother Joan had been less generous, often referring to Seth's girlfriend from college, Bethy Abramson, when Alison would come to dinner. Seth's brother Jeffrey would instruct Alison, telling her that, "we don't eat leavened bread on Passover." "I've converted," she would remind him, "I'm a Jew." "Well," he would say, "you're Jew-ish."

"This is great," said Tamara, and took Alison in a full embrace, something Alison suspected she would never get used to. There was a relentless hugging at the temple and even the services sometimes culminated with entwining each other's arms. Alison had gotten skilled as placing herself between Seth and Sophie on such occasions, "Really you're amazing," Alison tried hard not to personalize the statement which, she reminded herself, did not include the caveat "for a goy." Tamara had befriended Alison at Intergenerational Day and had hugged her then by way of introduction. The children had made books and presented them to the parents at a luncheon and assembly. Tamara's son told the story of his grandfather Jerry, whose life was saved by being kosher. He had been on an aircraft carrier and had skipped lunch because they had been serving pork chops that day. When the canteen was hit, the grandfather was on the other side of the ship, safe, spared. Alison had prepared blintzes for the assembly, using Sara's recipe and listened as Sophie described the time she spent on her grandparents' farm in Iowa, praying irrationally that there would be no mention of bacon or pigs.

Alison's decision to convert had not been hard; perhaps it had not been hard enough. She had not pined for children before she met Seth. She expected to have them, but the idea was remote, far off in a future she rarely imagined. She had a good job working as a segment producer for *60 Minutes* and she spent her time using her income, which was at the time all discretionary, on buying beautiful pieces of furniture for her apartment on Riverside; she was delighted to find jewel-colored seltzer bottles for her windows facing the Hudson, her chairs were draped with cashmere throws. When Seth first spent the night with her she awoke and watched him sleep and felt a kind of alarm. She walked to the kitchen and made herself warm milk, stepping softly so as not to wake the sleeping writer. His limbs were strewn across her bed, the light of the city in a wedge across his face, his blue-black curls against her pillow and the lashes on his closed eyes as long as a girl's. She stood with a mug of milk, warmed and sweetened with honey, held between her hands and she thought that he should never leave. She felt that he was her family, not found, but returned to her. She had never felt such a physical ease as she did in his company. She regarded the beverage of childhood that she had made and set it silently on the counter, then lifted the down quilt and the high-count cotton sheets and slipped in beside him, drawing herself close and shaping herself to his contour. When she awoke in the morning she wanted children.

Alison was unskilled at holding back and loved Seth generously from the start. He had let her know at dinner at Swagat on Amsterdam that when they married, his mother would expect her to convert. She cast her eyes down and made a study of tearing off a piece of Naan. "Are we getting married?" she'd asked without lifting her head. He had let her suffer for longer than he should have and then leaned across the table and lifting her chin, kissed her on the mouth. Taking her face in his hands he smiled at her as if he had fashioned her. When she told her own mother she intended to marry him, her mother had told Alison that she should convert, that it was the mother that was the heart of the family and that it must be of a piece. "You will be the one that teaches them who they are," her mother told Alison. She had held her daughter by the shoulders and tears formed at the edges of her eyes. Alison saw that it was a loss to her and remembered the grace they said at meals their hands held and heads bowed down.

Alison knew of a woman, a widow, who had taken classes to learn how to cook Jewish food so that she could entice and marry a Jewish man, laboring over brisket and perfecting her kugel to attract him. Alison had not chosen Seth by design. She felt, in a Jewish way of thinking, that they had been chosen for each other, that they were *beshert* and certainly Sophie was proof of that—Sophie, who was for her a source of pride and pleasure, pure *nachas*. Sophie was sure of herself in a way that Alison had never been. Alison pictured her daughter intrepid and gleeful as she climbed high up the structure in the Day School yard. The best, Alison thought, of each of them. The fact of her daughter had brought a kind of forgiveness for Alison's having not been born Jewish. Alison may have had the heart of a stranger, but Sophie was a Jew. And because Alison had converted before their marriage, Sophie was born a Jew. She went to a Jewish school. She could count in Hebrew and grew up in a home that had Shabbat on Friday and a menorah in the window on Chanukah. Alison worked hard to make a world for Sophie and the world she had made was Jewish.

Alison made challah, she made chicken soup floating with dill, she made latkes that were crisp and hot when she served them, unlike Leah Kaplan, who made hers the day before. For Purim, which was days away, Alison made hamantashen from a recipe of her own design—a dough with corn meal a filling with cherries that were tart and sweet. The other women gently teased her that she had made the time for such tasks, but it was her choice. It was her belief and her mother's too, that it was brave not weak to love another person. She had known many women in the community who cooked not at all, one who had a husband who was a vegetarian who came home each day from a day of work and would fend for himself. She believed that marriage was a shared narrative that you constructed together as you moved through each day. Her marriage—she knew—had been fortunate in the way that she and Seth were literally on the same page. They had a story that they told themselves and in the story, Alison was a Jew. There was no trace in their household of the Alison before, although it lingered in Alison and threatened the *Shalom Bayit* she had worked so hard to achieve.

In the story of their lives, Seth adored Alison. He could be caught looking at her and still catching his breath when she walked into a room. But in the years since Sophie was born, he attended to her differently. He worked now on a successful show that kept him away from the house until late. When in the past he had attended services with his wife and daughter, more often than not, it was for Alison alone to take Sophie to the sanctuary. Seth was less and less a part of their day and when, after working, he would return home without energy or attention for her, she discovered in herself a kind of anger that frightened her. She had done, she believed, what had been asked of her. She had taken her curiosity and intellect and embarked on a path of knowledge that she excelled at. She delved into her study and was not only an eager student, but the most eager. She invested in her study all the love of God she had felt in her home growing up. She had heard Rabbi Snow speak of one light, many lanterns. She but held a new lantern and her deep love of God illuminated it. But the truth was—and this truth was known only to her—she sometimes wished to return to the house of her childhood and to pray in the words she had used there.

The summer before the family had gone to Israel for the Bar Mitzvah of Seth's nephew Ari. They had walked the streets of the old city on a tour, arranged by his sister-in-law for the family on their fourteen-day junket. They had covered themselves with mud at the Dead Sea and walked through the chalky headstones in the Garden of the Fallen and had walked the streets of the old city. In Jerusalem, they were led through the narrow passages that were heavy with the fragrances of cumin and sage. They were led, in their hurried tour, to the Church of the Holy Sepulcre and stepping inside Alison was suddenly overcome. The air floated with frankincense and was made cool by the stone walls. Alison caught her breath. The room was ornate and shimmering with stunning frescoes with halos of real gold and, in the center, stood the stone of His Ascension. Alison had to cover her mouth with her hand, the air was so charged and expectant. The party listened with interest and as she stood before the rock where Jesus had been crucified. A hole invited you to touch the hallowed earth. Alison had to stay her own hand. As the guide described the history to the party, Alison's fingers searched the air, yearning. To avoid detection, she converted the gesture, and brought her hand to rest on Sophie's shoulder. When she returned home, she dreamed of the room again and again. When Alison's mother died, Seth and Sophie accompanied her to the service in the church she grew up in in Iowa. She held tight to Sophie's hand to keep firm her commitment, not taking communion but bowing her head instead.

Alison thought of marriage as a kind of religion, a state that required sacrifice and leaps of faith. She knew that many marriages were a struggle—two people competing for a resource that was ever dwindling—but she had given herself over to her marriage with a full heart and knew the very safety of her daughter depended on it. Each day that she entered the temple she struggled to find ease, sometimes instructing herself to inhale and exhale as if to fill her very lungs with the Judaism within the walls. It was to Sophie a second home. She skipped through the halls with ownership. In the sanctuary, she ran to the balcony to play with the other children without fear of reprisal by the rabbi who kept them in his line of sight.

Tamara tucked the donated basket into the cabinets they had designated for storage before the carnival. They had arranged for a slide and a moon bounce, and vendors to sell Hebrew National hot dogs and Chinese chicken salad, but the auction was consistently the biggest fundraiser and brought in some thirty thousand a year for the Day School scholarship fund. Alison was proud of her role in it and had found her dormant producer skills were useful in the task. "We'll meet again on Friday after drop-off," offered Tamara. Alison was entering the date into her iPhone when it rang in her hand. "Hello?" she held a finger up to Tamara, who indicated an invisible watch and that she had to go. The voice on the other end was frantic and hard at first to understand. "Alison this is Stephie from the Day School, Sophie's okay." Alison's body reacted at once and she tried to focus. "I'm here," she said. "Did somebody call you?" Stephie asked. The confusion lead to a further delay in understanding and Stephie asked, "How did you know?" "What is it?" Alison said, fighting to keep her voice from rising, walking now more briskly toward the classrooms where Sophie had gone to K through five. "Sophie fell, she's fallen." And Alison ran. Ran first to the office, where she found Stephie still holding the other end of the phone and then, following Stephie's waving arms down the back stairs to the yard. Alison saw her first through the upstairs window, the class and teachers in a horseshoe shaped tableau around a fallen Sophie, her head in the arms of her teacher, the yard aide pressing the rush of children back and away as they raised themselves on tip-toe to see her better. Sophie's skin was the color of snow, bloodless. The phone fell from Alison's hand and she was in five quick strides beside her daughter. She cradled her and began talking in a voice that betrayed nothing. "Hi Mommy," said Sophie, eyes wide. "Hi Baby," said Alison casual upbeat. "How's it going?" This earned Alison a smile, which she held while she ran the math of the height of the structure and the firmness of the concrete. "I fell," "Yeah yah did." and with that Sophie's head fell back and her muscles lost their hold. Alison grabbed her daughter more fiercely and demanded her consciousness.

Sophie moaned like a dreamer and Alison scolded her. "Sophie!" Her eyes opened. And Alison hoisted her. Alison came face to face with the

Day School principal, who seemed terrified as if calculating litigation. "Should we call an ambulance?" she asked weakly, Alison ignored her; she knew the distance to the Cedars, where Sophie had been born. She could be there in four minutes. Tamara was five strides ahead of Alison and ran to start the minivan.

Tamara navigated the LA grid with the skill of a carpooler and managed it with her head turned back to Alison who cradled Sophie in the back seat. Alison concentrated on fixing the attention of Sophie's eyes. She asked her questions she had been asked after a car accident she had had driving one winter on an icy road at home. "Do you know what day it is, Sophie?" "Fuck a bunch of you!" suggested Tamara to a clutch of drivers who impeded her progress. "Sorry, Sophie." "What day is it, honey?" Sophie said nothing and closed her eyes as if sleepy. Alison squeezed her shoulder and she came back to her. "Tuesday," she said, then, "because *Scrubs* is on." "Good girl," said Alison; the answer brought tears to her eyes. Tamara lay on the horn and crossed La Cienega at a diagonal. Sophie's eyes shut like a sleeper. "Who's the president, Baby?" Alison pressed her. A smile formed on her lips her eyes still closed. "O-ba-ma." Sophie's eyes opened and she looked straight at her mother as if to speak, and her eyes rolled back in her head. Alison felt the fabric of her daughter's t-shirt dampen. Tamara took the next turn riding over the curb. "We're here. We're here." Alison saw the white Star of David that identified Cedars as they rounded the corner to the Beverly Center. Tamara directed the van into the bay of the ER, threw the van into park, and ran around to open the door for Alison as she carried her daughter into the ER. "Call Seth." Alison called back to Tamara, as she ran with the child through the automatic doors. Alison was surrounded at once by people, calm in their urgency, who took her daughter from her arms and shifted her onto a cotton-sheeted gurney.

Seth arrived twenty minutes later with Ginny, his assistant, who used his iPhone to google the doctor, who performed the surgery to reduce the intracranial pressure resulting from the fall. Alison and Jeff waited in the Disney-sponsored pediatric waiting area and took turns making the short walk across the room, returning to each other to lay one hand over the other's. Seth twice called back east to tell his parents that they didn't know anything yet. Four hours later, the doctor stepped out of the cheerfully painted doors to tell them that Sophie was out of the woods and in recovery.

Later in the room they had assigned to Sophie, a plastic bag with her shoes and clothes on the sill, Seth and Alison gasped when their daughter briefly opened her dark eyes and spoke to them. For the next dozen hours, the couple took turns watching their daughter sleep. When it was Seth's turn, Alison stepped quietly out of the room to get him a Starbucks. She walked through the hall onto the plaza level and without intending to pulled open the heavy door and entered the chapel. The sound of the hospital receded behind her and she took a seat on one of the empty wooden pews. In the spare room—which offered, depending on the hour, the reassurances of both Rabbi and Priest—Alison sat alone trembling as her body registered the crisis averted, dropped her head in gratitude, and prayed.

Minyan

RAFE MENDELSSOHN needed a smoke. He patted the flattened pack in his jacket and felt a jolt of reassurance. He crossed the lobby to the hospital gift shop where he took his place in a long line behind a man jostling an oversized teddy bear like a father at a carnival. Rafe wondered whom the bear was for, the man's jaw set tight and eyes distant as if pleading. The children's wing was a place of murals and visiting clowns. Rafe remembered that clowns were universally feared by children and wondered when adults would get it right. The gift shop was populated with librarian-like volunteers in smocks, these women a population most easily seduced. Rafe purchased a roll of cherry Life Savers and a People magazine so he would have something to do with his hands. The lobby looked something like an airport, with large floor-to-ceiling windows and groupings of chairs for relatives waiting for news. At the center of the room was a grand piano being played by an older man with singular joyfulness, acting as his own page-turner of a fake book, playing "The Way You Look Tonight." Rafe faced the closed doors of the chapel and then turned away to overlook the courtyard, where someone else was smoking. He envied them the way you would the owner of a beautiful home or the husband of a beautiful wife.

Upstairs Rafe's father was allegedly dying. Rabbi Beth had gotten a call from Charleze, his father's wife, and had been informed that he had a wish to see Rafe and Rafe had gotten as far as this lobby. There was a Starbucks on this floor and he had meant only to stop for a latte, but he had stayed, sinking into the chair nearest the piano and remaining there. He had no intention of going upstairs but neither could he leave. And so he had lingered like a passenger delayed and had camped nearly three hours in the lobby on the second floor.

He knew what was expected of him, though Rabbi Beth had exerted no pressure. She had only passed along the message and in truth she had done so tentatively. Her eyes cast down, her pretty dark hair falling over the bridge of her nose, she had patted the sleeve of his suit and told him the decision was all his. But her gesture was tinged with apology as if asking an actor to work for less than scale.

Rafe thought of the way the scene with his father would play in one of his movies. He knew that in the third act, he would enter his father's hospital room and there would be a revelation. His father would struggle for air, and in a speech both poignant and witty he would address all hurts and wrongs. There was no language that could correct what had been taken from Rafe. This man was not entitled to the relief of Rafe's forgiveness. Rafe would not be available for this task of an errand boy. Let his other family bring him ice chips and pat his brow.

When his father died Rafe intended to sue his family for his money. Not because he needed money; he did not. But because he believed that everything that family believed to be theirs was his. He calculated his loss in many terms but the easiest to measure was the money. The last time he saw his father was over a lunch orchestrated by the relentlessly hopeful Ariel. Abe had remarked without irony that he had had "a good life" and Rafe was gobsmacked. Abe said this as if to reassure them, as if they had left him, a squalling infant, on the steps of a church. Abe was already seventy and harmless but this insult mattered to Rafe. On whose back had he had a good life, at whose expense? He had agreed to the lunch because of his sister, because it mattered to her and she mattered to Rafe. Ariel, who would be dashed to the rocks by a wave, and right herself, to be dashed again. He left the lunch vowing to never see his father again, a threat that went completely undetected by Abe in the ensuing decade, until yesterday when his wife Charleze conveyed the request. Rafe struggled to believe her willingness to do so; her treasure so closely guarded, he found it hard to imagine her careless now.

Rafe returned to his seat and, crossing his legs, studied his shoe. It was beautifully made from leather, designed as well as an Italian car. He had more than one pair; twelve lined up in his closet like guardians of the twenty-five beautiful suits. He had eight cashmere coats. In what approximated winter in L.A., Rafe would don the camelhair and walk around the pool. The navy Burberry, he would spread like a blanket on the grass and set the lovely white ass of a girl from craft services on the gold satin lining inside. Rafe had everything he wanted. He had outstripped the need for a father, making a world for himself that was safe in all ways, and could not think of why he needed to attend to him now, why he needed to make a play of it that ended with forgiveness. And yet he could not leave.

The pianist had begun to believe himself the object of Rafe's interest. The barista also eyed him over the nonfat double half-caf, but Rafe only stayed because of a commandment he could not reconcile. To honor his father. He felt it was possible, after all, that the sin was his. That he was obligated to test it. And he had gotten as close as he could to his dying father and waited to know.

Rafe had gotten a text on his cell from Rabbi Beth. She had heard that his father was at Cedars from the chaplain, Rabbi Meier and had texted for him to call if he needed to talk. She had closed with the offer of a *"Mi sheberach,"* which it pleased him to imagine her typing in with slender fingers. He thought of Rabbi Beth and remembered her dressed as a cheerleader at the Purim Shpeil. He felt a pleasant flash of guilt at the thought. She was certainly not the rabbi of Rafe's youth, bearded and over-sincere. A man not interested in assuming the vacant role of Rafe's father despite the tireless efforts of Rafe's mother, who felt the disappointment she had in all men more acutely in this spiritual leader who wasn't.

Rafe saw the door to the chapel open. The chaplain, also bearded but with a thoughtful face, leaned out and let a man in. Inside Rafe saw other men, standing and seated, crane around to account for the newcomer. The door was quickly shut after and Rafe's attention was drawn to a lovely volunteer with strawberry-blonde hair. "Magazine?" She turned her head and paged through the stack of magazines on her cart, reading the titles playfully. "Sunset magazine has a new recipe for salsa and tips on how to refinish your deck?" Rafe could bring flirting to any dialogue. "I could use some deck tips," he said and nearly landed her. The volunteer blushed and made work of reordering her stack. She passed him the magazine and, composing herself, said, "I hope things work out," not knowing if he were meting the time while a mother had a hip replaced or a daughter had a skin graft. Her offer was saturated with actual kindness and Rafe knew at once that she had sat in these chairs waiting. "Thank you," he said and gifted her, saying, "I'm sure it will." He held her gaze until she walked away, smiling and shaking her head.

Rafe closed his eyes and laid his head back against the chair. He pictured the gathering around of his father's other family. Abe's oldest, Aaron, he knew had adopted an infant with his partner. He had read this on Facebook when an algorithm suggested that he and Aaron might become "friends." Perhaps they had brought the toddler along. He imagined the family as they would be seen by a passerby, so sad and beautiful. Rafe was unable to place himself in the picture. An unpleasant sympathy rose in Rafe's chest imagining the portrait of Abe and his grandchild. He pushed it quietly aside. What did he owe these strangers? Nothing, he reasoned. They had his father, which was more than enough. Later Rafe would call his sister and she alone would understand the relief his father's death might bring. The father who did not acknowledge them. Who was able to until this day think about them not at all. The chaplain opened the door a second time, this time leaning with the weight of it and falling outward, looking first down one hallway and then its opposite. He consulted his watch and, repeating his glance in both directions, he closed the door and returned to his gathering congregation.

Rafe walked to the windows that ran floor-to-ceiling and peered out. From where he stood he could see the trail of smoke rising from the hand of a woman who seemed to be considering a spot on the pavement. A man spoke to her but Rafe judged that it was not her spouse.

Their smoke in the stairwell seemed intimate. The woman held her slender wrist up and away from her body, letting the smoke drift up. While Rafe watched, the man closed the gap and pressed himself into her body. She kept her hand and the cigarette extended in midair but yielded to him. After the kiss she broke and looked up and away. Rafe was proved right. The woman was a cheater. Her husband was likely somewhere in the rooms across the way—which Rafe could also see—bleeding out.

Rafe watched another scene play out below. A surgical nurse in dark purple scrubs talking instructively on her cell phone, also smoking, pacing and putting her cigarette out in a planter, aggressively screwing the remaining filter into the dry dirt. Each scene made a story for him like the movies he made. He knew the beauty and importance of gesture. In an editing room he might have watched the turn of the wrist of the adulterous wife over and over and over.

Rafe turned away from the glass and across the room was face to face once again with the chaplain. He appeared to be looking directly at him as if considering him, taking his measure. "Forgive me." Rafe was interrupted by a man about his age. "I'm sorry, but are you still reading that People?" "I am not." Rafe realized he had become a fixture, had paced the lobby long enough to have been observed. "Take it," he offered. "Help yourself," he added in a way that made the man blush a little, as if Rafe had given him a present. "Thank you," he stammered. "It's been a long night." Rafe recognized this salvo, this invitation to step into the man's narrative, and urgently wanted to move away. At once he was hardened to the concerns of this stranger. He did not want to know that upstairs the man's father was ailing. Rafe did not want to hear about how they had all loved him. Rafe could care less. He found this affection unctuous and weak. He would have none of it. "Keep the magazine," Rafe said and took a strong stride away. "It's all yours."

The steps he took put him closer to the door of the chapel. The chaplain, he saw, was gesturing to him. Rafe looked instinctively over his shoulder, expecting that the gesture was not meant for him but for someone just behind him. But the chaplain poked at the air directly at

Rafe. Rafe took clumsy steps toward him as if walking into the breach of cold water.

"Are you Jewish?" The chaplain said this in a conspiratorial whisper, drawing his arm around Rafe's shoulder like a carney coaxing him into a tent. Rafe felt instinctively suspicious, as if he were being asked his mother's maiden name and social security number. He said nothing. The chaplain grew impatient. "Are you Jewish?" Then, as if Rafe were a sleepyheaded boy in *cheder*, instructed, "for Mincha." He indicated his watch. "I need a tenth man." Rafe took a full step back as if affronted but the door swung open and the chaplain strode in, so Rafe followed.

Rafe sat behind a man he recognized as Steven Spielberg. The other eight men were mostly older but all familiar, as if they had pulled Rafe's contact list and invited his dentist and his lawyer and his tax attorney. Some of the men, surgeons, were dressed in scrubs. The rabbi made his way to the compact *bima* that stood on thin legs at the front of the room like a sample case and began Mincha. "*Ashrai yoshvei be'techa...*" Rafe opened the bound prayer book and for the first time today knew what to do. He let the book fall open in his hand and traced the black letters on the smooth white pages. The men went about the business of prayer. Rafe liked that there were no women and became keenly aware of the relief he felt at the exclusion of their company. He brought the prayer book to his face and smelled the pages, the leather binding smooth in his palm and weighted in his hand.

The man beside him wept. He did this unselfconsciously and generously in a way that made Rafe know that he had lost his beloved bride. Rafe placed his hand under the man's elbow to steady him and the man lowered to his seat. The man took out a white handkerchief from his pocket and produced a blustery blow. Rafe remained standing and felt the lock step of his fellows as they recited each prayer. Upstairs, he thought, my father is dying. He knew this in his body, the way that your bones feel the dusk. He knew also that he would not go to him and a simple relief took him over. Rafe lowered to his seat and rested. He looked over his father's life like a movie played in reverse.

And Rafe knew that while it was sad that Abe had not been a father to him, that Abe was not able or brave, that it was saddest of all for Abe. That it was the story of Abe Mendelssohn that was ending today. That around him, the strangers who he had made a family would mourn him, would lean on each other and hover at his bedside. They would collect the flowers and plants that had been staged on the window at the edge of the sink like a set dresser breaking down a scene.

Abe Mendelssohn's story was ending. And the people that were meant to weep for him, Rafe and Ariel, did not even know him. Did not know the smell of his skin when they leaned in to kiss his dry lips. Did not know the clean smell of soap on his hands. In the story of Abe Mendelssohn the characters who would have been his son and his daughter were the strangers now. The chaplain asked all who were saying *Kaddish* for their deceased relatives to rise and Rafe did. Because, while he could not make a play of bending at his father's bedside and saying a poignant goodbye, this he could do.

Tiyul

RABBI BETH SAT in the driver's seat of her Prius with the door open and traded her flats for her Nikes, double-knotting them against un-raveling so they would remain secure for her hike up Fryman. She had left work early. Returning from Sova, the food pantry, where she had bagged groceries with the Day School's fourth grade, Beth had called from the car to let Marilyn know she would be out for the remainder of the day. The secretary would assume that Beth was making a *shiva* call or a stop at Cedars, but instead Beth had driven over Laurel Canyon to Fryman Canyon to hike. Beth pulled up to the entrance of the public park, stepped out of her car and produced the three-dollar parking fee. The bills were worn and Beth gingerly fed them into the "iron ranger," a skill she perfected in the coin-operated Laundromat at Barnard. The Lexus behind her honked loudly; there was no such thing as waiting in L.A.

Beth locked her purse in the trunk of the Prius and noted that hers was the green one, the parking lot looking something like a dealership for the politically correct car. She crossed the lot past pairs of middle-aged women, actors, and personal trainers, nearly all with dogs strain-ing to begin up the trail, pulling at their leashes to return to nature.

Beth took a preemptive sip of water and started up the hardest part of the hike; the first fifty yards were steep and lined with tall eucalyptus trees that scented the air like a sauna. The first push up the slope en-gaged all of Beth's body, her breath her singular focus, her calves push-ing away the earth to ascend; the rest of the trail was more forgiving.

The day had been long and Beth hoped to spend the sadness and despair that she had taken in. In the morning she had received news that not one but *two* of the Day School mothers had been diagnosed with breast cancer. This had prompted a flurry of activity: the room parents, Marcus and Elliot, the dads of twins in the preschool, racing to coordinate food delivery to the ailing women; Marilyn slating the women for calls from the Sisterhood and adding their names to the *Mi sheberach* list for Friday night's services; the other Day School mothers hastening to their homes to schedule mammograms and Google BRCA.

Later, Beth had seen Mara, the sixth grader who had lost her mother to the same plague two years before. The child had grown tall and had the unique posture of an orphaned daughter, her shoulders drawn down against the yearning height of her own body. Mara had washed her hands for too long at the sink and turned to Beth, who was drying hers on the looping cloth towel. "Sucks to be them," the child had quipped and just as quickly had collapsed in tears.

Beth had comforted Mara in the ways that she knew how and returned the child to class, better for now. The girl's Bat Mitzvah study would begin soon and there would be a place to shape her hope. Beth envisioned her a year away at the *bima* standing with a straightened spine.

Beth reached the top of the slope where the vista was of the much-maligned San Fernando Valley, beautiful from where she stood overlooking it through a thatch of wild pomegranate trees that clung to the hillside. A duo of Day School mothers huffed by and Beth used a slug of water to signal that she was not available to talk. She caught the tail of their conversation as they pushed past, "highly gifted...magnet points." Beth stretched her calves and gave them the lead. The trail was busy this time of day, when in some other cities, people sat at desks. This occupation of Los Angelinos was a kind of employment— staying fit and attractive, staying sane.

Beth rounded the trail and was caught by the fragrance of sage that transported her to the hills around Jerusalem. She shut her eyes and felt the cool air on her skin. Tears sprouted from her eyes and she dropped to her knees. She was the girl who had lost her mother and felt throughout the ache of missing her. How is a girl meant to grow in a world so dangerous and hard? Why must she wake in the dark from a dream without a mother to call out to? Beth's palms pressed into the damp earth and she rose. She wiped her eyes on the hem of her t-shirt and resumed her trek. Her congregation was wracked with pain and Beth's hike had only just started.

It had been a hard year for Beth's community, hard in new ways. The epidemic of breast cancer was not new, although it was novel to the women that received the news. The shock at being so chosen, the bad lottery, the terrifying fear of leaving their children. And like in every congregation there was loss in all forms, some having the suggestion of logic and fairness—the death of old men and old women from age and from time. Others that seemed like the act of a petulant God—a singer with throat cancer, a groom who dies on the day of his wedding, a man, who, while casting his sins in the ocean at *tashlich*, slips in the water and severs his spine. "Who by fire, who by water?" When Beth looked out at the congregation she saw each family captioned in this way and her heart broke for them.

This year she saw men and women who were fearful. Where before there had been *parnasa*, an abundance that allowed every woman and man to feel generous, this year her congregants were struggling in ways that they had not predicted. The "business" had retracted and the parents in the Day School came in secret, one after another, to make arrangements to pay tuition, borrowing from their pensions and from their parents. Marriages were strained by the uncertainty. "The roof leaks and we cannot fix it," said the wife of a television writer, her voice shredding with fear, as if the damage were not to their house in Hancock Park, but to the thatched roof of their home in the *shteytl*, a breach that had let in a cold winter wind. The men sat beside congregants who could help them and yet they did not speak for their shame. "The only way to get help in this town is to *not* need it," said an aging director who sat in her office, his head in his hands. Never had they dreamed that the gleanings in the field might be gathered for them.

Beth measured her steps by her breath. The sun broke through the leaves but it was cool in the shade. The seasons in L.A., which people on the east coast seemed not to believe in, shifted in subtle, almost undetectable ways. Winter was marked by the appearance of Meyer lemons on the small tree that grew outside Beth's kitchen door. Spring was signaled by the faint jasmine on the air at night when Beth slept with the window just opened.

At the food pantry this morning, Beth had asked the children to imagine what it would mean to manage with only the food in the bag. To find yourself grateful to have your arms weighed down with groceries, cans of green beans and tuna, a kind of soup that was not your favorite. "I'd just order risotto from Pinot," supplied the son of the board member who had sat in the high-backed chairs on the *bima* on Yom Kippur. Beth knew that this child would suffer if his world changed—this child who had never had a green bean from a can, who was prepared for nothing but everything.

As a form of repair she thought of Levi, a child with a heart so open he was in danger. The children had been filling their bags with tuna, and beans, and soup, and she saw that he appeared stuck, his hand wrapped tight around a can he held out in front of him. Beth faced him and saw his brow furrowed as if in study, tears shimmering, just held in by the levee of his lower lid, the tiny lashes moistened to peaks like a child's drawing of the sun. Beth had placed her hand on his shoulder and he re-started. She knew that his heart was weighted with the thought of the other child, the one who would receive this food. He had extended his hand in an offering of canned corn and had met his twin who lived in a world without. Beth had had to unfurl his small fingers, releasing his grip.

Beth rounded the corner and reached the point in the trail where the city was no longer visible, an illusion that made her feel for a moment that she stood on the edge of the earth, the sky wide and relentless. The wind was loud in her ears, shutting out all other sound. A shuddering sigh left her body. Beth's arms dropped at her sides and her hands fell open, as if a moment before, each held a stone.

Beth started up the rise of the path that faced west. There, a house was nestled in the hills that seemed certainly imperiled. Beth calculated that the house was one mudslide or brush fire or earthquake from destruction. It was arrogant and flaunting itself on the edge of Mulholland, and Beth stood as if waiting for it to tumble down the hill. The sun warmed her shoulders as it lowered in the sky. She thought of the two mothers at home waiting. Each in her house, arranging her calendar to prepare her children and husband for her absence. In the coming days fielding the affection and the stark anxiety of the women that would cross her threshold. The visitors, who were enjoined to visit the sick, arriving with cupcakes and scented lotion and leaving with shame for the deep relief they felt that this time they were spared.

Beth took the next leg of the hike with more intention. She wanted the work to feel hard in her sinews. She wanted her lungs to smart. The earth was broken and the path dropped off in places where it had been worn away by winter rain. Beth pushed herself harder. She was the father who could not pay his son's tuition and he was deeply ashamed. He kept secret from his wife that their savings had long been pilfered and that the deal he was hoping to secure had fallen through. He watched the mail for the green envelopes that brought residuals and prayed, prayed to God, that they would be enough to buy him time before it all fell apart. His wife learned of this when her cell phone stopped working and again when she went to pay for sushi and her card had been declined. In Beth's office, seated across from her on the sofa, the man's wife had moved away from, not toward him, when he wept. His wife stood up and left the room.

Beth reached the summit and vomited. She crouched over the high grass and pressed the back of her hand to her mouth. She stood and rinsed her mouth with water from the bottle and spit it out over the ledge. She pulled her hair back in a ponytail and secured it with a rubber band from her pocket. The vista now was at its most beautiful. The hills shimmered with silver grass. The dark greens in the deepest part of the valley had turned to blue with the waning sun. At Beth's heels a dog lapped from the cool water at the fountain that had been built at the site in loving memory of Sylvia Rosenblum and Buster.

Beth took the rest of the path at a run, letting gravity and her own speed propel her forward, landing hard with each footfall. She stopped still when she saw the deer, Beth's chest still rising and falling with her effort. Beth made herself quiet and steadied her breathing. The animal's eyes were like dark glass as they rounded to look at Beth and, finding her not a threat, gave permission imperceptibly to two velvet fawns that they may follow. Beth held her body in stillness and awe. Relieved, she measured her own heartbeat and matched it to the beating heart in the white chest of the doe.

The Ethical Will of Henya Wallenberg

HENYA WALLENBERG SAT at the kitchen table of her apartment on Rosewood and considered the ethical will she attempted to compose. "Dearest children," she began. With this she pictured them, not as the adults they were, but each at an age that exemplified them. The lives of her children flickered in her memory like a zoetrope. On the top of the page, on a stenographer's pad, in the excellent handwriting that was demanded of her childhood, Henya had written. "People are capable of unspeakable evil." She thought that perhaps she would save this truth for later in the document. Although she knew that to deny this truth was dangerous, that to live with it also dangerous, exhausting. She began again. "Make books your companions," she tried. She thought that this advice had wisdom and imagined each of her children reading with great pleasure, being parented in her absence by the writers of great books. Finally, she settled on, "Treat all people with respect." She remembered then the painful deference of her neighbor's maid Adi, a *schvartza*. She had come to help Henya after Michael was born and Henya recalled her taking instruction with her held tilted down, as if reading the words from the linoleum floor. Henya had taken her hand and the maid, Adi, had startled at the touch. Henya had brought her to the table and served her sweet tea and *kichel*. "Treat all people with respect," she wrote. How easy the habit to treat others as less, how enticing. Here in LA it was the Latina housekeeper, the men who brought the Lexus to her son after dinner. "Be honest in your dealings with others," Henya wrote. Simple, she thought, but not easy. Her daughter Dara practiced at being manipulative first, honest second, a reaction to having been deceived herself, a preemptive strike, a child that she loved, but sometimes did not like. Though beautiful and successful, she had few female friends, did not know how to have them. Henya wished she could instruct her to "have friends." Henya thought of the days, when without her own friends, she would have crumbled. Henya remembered her friend Julia standing at the doorway of her bedroom. "You're inside out," she had said, and without another word she had sat down beside Henya and wrapped her arms fiercely around her, like a frame for her, and had literally held her up. "You will not die of despair," Henya added, "you will only wish to." And with this, Henya recalled the loss of her husband, and the living loss of her son. "Pray." She added and again, "Pray."

Henya had brought the children to the temple in the early sixties when Rabbi Rabinowitz was on the pulpit. Rabbi Snow had not come until Aaron's Bar Mitzvah. The rabbi had children of his own now, twins, already in college. Henya had seen them, tall now, when they came home for the holidays to blow the *shofar*; one in the sanctuary, the other in the chapel. There had been no women on the *bima* when she had first joined Beth Shalom. It had been a struggle for Henya to wrap herself in a *tallit* and take an *aliyah* for her granddaughter's Bat Mitzvah. Her tradition had been Orthodox, but the temple itself had attracted her, the very stone of the walls. She wanted her children to know how to pray, because you don't know what will come. She thought of her own prayers and knew at once that she had ever only prayed for her own strength. She had grown up with a fatherly God, but learned from her own father that man is God, that our conduct is holy or not, honest or not, that it is incumbent upon us to free the captive and to heal the sick.

"Give *tzedakah*" and with this, she meant to think of others outside of yourself. She thought suddenly of Chava, the volunteer at Thalians, who cared for her son. It was rare that she saw him without her. She spoke to the piece of him that remained, that remembered himself. She lay her hand on his in silence when remembering himself broke his own heart, when his eyes darted from place to place, unable to alight. The volunteer was a friend to him. "Treat people with respect." She repeated. She had boundless gratitude to Chava, whose own daughter had been murdered in her dorm room at college. "People are capable of unspeakable evil." Henya stopped and felt the burden of what she knew about the world. She thought of her grandchild, Sadie, and it lifted her. She wished that her parents were able to see her as she did. Her son and his wife imagined the child immune to their fighting when she is only inured to it. "Repair the world." Henya sat with her pen poised and remembered with great joy the days with her husband when their time was well spent, a public defender using his keen mind and intellect to make the protection of the law true. Henya sat in the back of the courtroom finding beauty in his language. Handsome to her in his intention and commitment—the real thing. She ached for him and remembered what were the sweetest days of their lives, their salad days; all three children, under ten, sitting at the table of their kitchen, being quizzed by their father on democracy, the system of checks and balances, Aaron rewarding his father with thoughtful reflection, a heart as tender as new grass. Aaron. Henya shaped her son's name and drew her robe more tightly.

It was his first year of college at Columbia when they had gotten the call, Ben on the phone in his office and Henya on the extension in the kitchen, blue with a long cord so that she could talk while cooking dinner. Aaron had said that he believed his food to be poisoned. Henya remembered with clarity the unreality of the call; the remark bookended with cogent and remarkable observations about the world. Ben had asked him to repeat what he had said about the food and Henya had laid the phone down on a potholder on the counter and had walked into Ben's office. Ben had remained on the phone and spoke to his son with reassurance, telling him he would be there soon. Henya had stood at the doorway and they had looked at each other with the measure of their understanding uncensored. She had come to his side and held his free hand in both of hers. Ben had remained in New York for five months until the hospital released him and allowed him to fly home with Ben at his side—Aaron, like a child who had woken in the night, and sleepwalking, was directed gently back to his room. They had found a bed for him at Cedars, where the medication diminished the hallucinations but also the attention and clarity that made it possible for Aaron to read. All pleasures were robbed from him. Rabbi Meier, the hospital chaplain, who visited on weekends, would wrap a *tallis* around both their shoulders and in a chair at the end of his bed, they would pray. And Aaron would respond to the familiar melodies and with a voice that was quiet, discuss the weekly Torah portion, the intellectual rigor of the exercise sometimes bypassing the haze of medications for moments.

Henya recalled the rest she felt with Ben when she lay on the top of the covers in the evening, the lights off, her head on his chest, his arm lightly across her waist. They had a ritual of reviewing the day before Henya would rise to get the children ready for bed and Ben would return to his office to write briefs and research his cases. The ritual persisted after the children had grown. She had not believed herself capable of living without him and had not intended to.

"Love generously," she began, and thought with gratitude of the fearlessness with which she had loved her husband. She believed this to be the gift of their youth. Growing up together; Ben unpracticed at dissembling, grieved unguardedly when he received the call that his beloved sister had died. Sitting on a chair in the kitchen with his head dropped, Henya took the phone from his hand and returned it to its cradle. She sat on floor beside him and had known it would be false and an injury to console him with words.

Ben relied on Henya for counsel in his fatherhood. And she knew her own beauty in his appreciation of it, catching his breath on the rare occasion she would apply lipstick for a wedding or Bar Mitzvah. They loved each other simply. Were kind. She had seen in the marriage of her son Michael a kind of competition, the pair miserly with their energy as if afraid of losing ground; the house never filled with the enticing air of a waiting dinner. Her daughter-in-law, both bright and accomplished; her son, successful and respected, but neither Henya suspected, in love. She sensed between them a brokered partnership. Sadie, their miraculous daughter, was the best of them, unjaded and forgiving. Henya thought she might grow to be a rabbi or a judge. The child had her grandfather's *sitzfleish,* her attention sustained and intelligent, her heart most fair. Henya wished most that Ben might have known her for the pure *nachas* he would have felt.

When Henya married Ben, she had never kissed him or even held his hand. Ben had been the older brother of her best friend Tanya. Both of their families had been killed and they married so that there was a family. Ben had looked steadily at her and they married, because there was only a future. Tanya became her sister and they lived together, sharing the cooking and doing laundry. "Eff U En E X—Have you any eggs? They would tease. "Ess, Ess, I eff ex." They made a new world in the kitchen. Walking in the street with Tanya's arm tucked into her own, patting it as they did, to mark a rhythm, *we are here, we are here, we are still here.* When Tanya married Zev and moved with him to San Francisco, Ben and Henya spent their first night alone in the apartment and Michael was conceived with courage and intention. Their shared memory never spoken of, but the children named for the brother and mother and father they had lost: *Dovid, Malka. Avner— Dara, Michael, Aaron.* People are capable of unspeakable evil, she thought and recalled against her wishing the cold clay eyes of human hatred, feeling anew the shock of what men will do to answer their own weakness, shaping the fumes of their fear into violence, willing to punish with invention, novel in every moment, to devise new ways to tear flesh from bone. Henya pinched the flesh of her palm to return to the room. Steadying her breath, she guided her memory to the eyes of her sister Sarah, bright in a world before, when they lay together in the sun-warmed grass, their slender fingers intertwined.

Henya rose. Setting aside her papers, she lay her pen down carefully so that it would not roll. She took the teapot from the stove and, toggling the spout open, she filled it at the sink. She listened to the sound of the water running as if it were the voice of a companion. When she shut the water there was no sound. She crossed to the stove and listened to the tic tic tic of the pilot light, the blue flame rushing and heating the water. Henya stood without waiting. She opened a tin filled with Wissotzky tea and the fragrance reminded her of her mother's samovar. She thought too of the polish she rubbed on it with a soft cloth at Passover. She remembered this room when it was filled with her children. Dara, relentless and funny, pulling at Michael and Aaron cradling a grasshopper, making of his hands a shadow box. Ben was filling his cup with coffee and Henya, using the flat of a butter knife, tried to pry a waffle from roof of the waffle iron. Henya had caught the eye of her husband and both, without instruction, had set down what they held in their hands and stepped to each other. He slipping his hand to the small of her back and, drawing her fast to his side, they had stood facing the children, who stopped for the change in the room's air. All three looked up expectantly. And Ben had kissed her open-mouthed and eyes opened and the children had come from their seats at the table and crowded in.

Acknowledgments

I wish to express my deep appreciation to all those whose support gave shape to these stories.

My family Erica, Dean, Aram, and Rose whose faces I see still reflected in the living room window when we light candles.

Jon Shestack and Portia Iversen whose friendship and brisket have sustained me.

Amy Brotslaw Schweiger for support that began long before these pages were written.

Nadine Epstein, Anita Diamant, Erica Jong, *Moment Magazine*, and the Karma Foundation for their extraordinary support, which came at just the right time.

Susan Ginsburg at Writers House for her help in bringing these stories to light.

Erika Dreifus, Joan Gelfand, Nora Gold, Bob Goldfarb, Andrew Tonkovich, Rabbi Michael Lerner, Daniel E. Levenson and Yona Zeldis McDonough for making a place for Jewish short fiction.

Marla Frazee, Hannah Friedman, Ellie Herman, Ken Kwapis, Marisa Silver, Marla Strick, Jill Soloway, Sheldon Larry, and Heidi Levitt each for their talent and for their thoughtful reading of the stories.

Daniel Greenberg for his belief and encouragement.

Marie Brazil, Karen Jacobson, Julie Paris, Deirdre Sullivan, Jainee Patrice, and Lev and Barb Gonick for their love and support.

Jeff Bernhardt, Rachel Heller, Sherry Langer, Kevin Larkin, Liz Leshin, Tim Ryan Meinelschmidt, Mara Sperling, Karen Young, and Katie Zanecchia each for your role in being part of this work.

Cantor Aviva Rosenbloom for the meaning and heart she brings to prayer.

Rabbi Levi Meier ZT"L who gave us hope when hope was fleeting.

Will Deutsch and Charlotte Strick for bringing their substantial talent to bear on my behalf.

And to my husband, Karl Schaefer, for his unwavering support, his keen insight and humor, and for putting up the Sukkah.

Biography

RACELLE ROSETT is the winner of both the Moment Magazine-Karma Foundation Prize for Jewish short fiction and the Lilith Fiction Prize. Her work has also appeared in *Tikkun, Ploughshares,* the *New Vilna Review, Jewish Fiction,* the *Santa Monica Review,* and *Zeek.* As a television writer she won the WGA award for *thirtysomething.* She lives in Los Angeles with her husband and two sons. www.racellerosett.com

17733304R00084

Made in the USA
Lexington, KY
24 September 2012